Mafia Romance

Mafia Romance

MELVIN MCILVEEN

iUniverse

MAFIA ROMANCE

iUniverse books may be ordered through booksellers or by contacting:

iUniverse
1663 Liberty Drive
Bloomington, IN 47403
www.iuniverse.com
844-349-9409

ISBN: 978-1-4620-4963-9 (sc)
ISBN: 978-1-4620-5029-1 (e)

Print information available on the last page.

iUniverse rev. date: 07/14/2022

This book is dedicated to
my wife Dorothy Schofield McIlveen
who lived very close to an Italian Prisoner of
War Camp in Northern England
during the 1939-45 War.

This romance happens between an enterprising Italian activist and a beautiful young Yorkshire maiden who meet under unusual circumstances during the last great war.

The Italian is a prisoner of war who is forced to work in a British rural industry under skies which thunder with the sound of Bomber aircraft night after night during the hostilities as the war is brought to the home front in all of the countries of Europe in 1945.

The Italian prisoner meets and falls in love with a lass from a Yorkshire town which closely resembles the area where I met and married a Yorkshire lass myself while serving in the Canadian Air Force during that war.

Here, however, this fictional story is totally unlike my experience. A holiday spent in Italy some thirty years after the war has inspired this novel. The culture of Italy pervades this story. The Mafia and the conflict between the communist influences and the democratic movement which succeeded the Mussolini regime battle for supremacy.

Italy is a brutal, interesting, historic, and astonishing country.

Contents

▼

CHAPTER ONE

▼

THE PRISON CAMP

England had settled into the grim business of war by the year 1943. She had survived the blitz, and all the disappointments of the original battlefield defeats, in fact she had managed to convince all of her citizens and many in the occupied countries too of her eventual victory. The campaign in North Africa was going well and the flood of Italian prisoners of war, brought home to work in the farms of England was welcome respite for the beleagured farmers. This is the story of a romance which began in wartime England in 1943, which blossomed in spite of the nationality difference, and the language difficulties, between the Italian war prisoner and his Yorkshire girl friend.

My story opens with two young 17 year old English girls who having just passed their entrance examinations for college, are walking one evening along the bridle path which borders the west side of the manor house grounds in their village of Harrowdale, Yorkshire. The manor house was the home of the Howard family, owners of the cloth mill which is the largest employer in the area. Before the war, large parties would be held in these grounds for summer garden parties, or to celebrate important events such as the coronations or weddings of the Royal Family. July the Fourth, Independence day to the Americans, was celebrated also because Lady Howard was an American.(She had been a dancer in New York, it was whispered.) Many of these gatherings could be heard and spied upon from the bridle path, and the girls often came here when they were much younger to secretly look in on the adult garden parties.

Of late, Mary Holdwell and Gloria Bottomley had used the bridle path for its solitude. The Howards had left the manor house when the German planes had started coming over. Lady Howard had gone to Scotland to stay with friends while her husband had taken a position with the war ministry in London. The manor stood deserted for two years, then had been requisitioned by the government to house Italian prisoners of war who had volunteered to work in the Yorkshire farm lands. Mary Holdwell and Gloria Bottomley had become accustomed to using the bridle path when they wished to share secrets with each other. An affair of the heart, or just a need to talk of important things, such as one another's opinion of a particular new boy in the neighbourhood, or even of the latest cinema, was used as an occasion for a walk together along the bridle path.

At first there had been a certain boldness attached to these walks on the bridle path, for German planes would be flying over to drop their bombs on the industrial areas of Leeds and Bradford. By the year 1943, the sky was still filled with the sound of bombers overhead, but these were formations of British, Canadian, and American squadrons assembling for their nightly raids over Germany. Yorkshire was no longer the target, it was the trigger now.

The girls sat on their favourite stone seat together close to the manor gates, looking up to admire the huge formations in the sky.

Suddenly a tenor voice could be heard faintly over the hum of the bombers high above, and Mary at once recognized the song. "It's from Aida, it's a Verdi opera," she whispered. Suddenly a chorus of voices broke into song, drowning out completely the sound of the planes above.

"Oh, that's the chorus! Isn't it beautiful!"

"I guess so," said Gloria, "though I can't imagine it being sung by those greasy Eye-ties," She pulled her sweater around her shoulders, holding the collar tightly, and tucking her arms underneath. "Let's go home Mary, I'm getting cold."

Mary was dressed in a warm tweed coat, belted at the waist. She had not bothered to fasten the buttons, however, and the coat bottom swung open to reveal a bright red dress with a short knee length skirt. The blue and dark red colours of the tweed contrasted sharply and complemented the bright red of her dress. Her blonde hair was neatly arranged in a Page Boy coiffure of curls which rested comfortably on the collar of her coat.

"I want to hear more, Gloria. It's beautiful singing! Better than I've heard at the Palladium in Leeds, by far. Let's listen just a little while longer, please."

"If we wait any longer, one of those Eye-ties is liable to come down the path and see us, and if they were to catch us alone in here, there's no telling what they would do to us. They're prisoners of war, you know. They've been kept locked up here for six months. OOOOH, I bet they wouldn't half like to get a girl down in the woods here! Coom on Mary, let's get home."

The chorus singing died out and the girls rose to leave the grounds. There was a rustle of branches from across the pathway and two men in brown battle dress emerged from the woods.

They were prisoners from the compound above, who had been out for a stroll themselves.

Mary stood still her hand on her breast, while Gloria cried out in alarm. The men knew full well that they had startled the two girls and they fell to their knees as if to apologize. their hands raised, palms outstretched in a gesture of surrender.

"You better not touch me," said Gloria, "my brother's in the Eighth Army and he'll do for you, proper like, if you so much as touch me!"

Mary had to smile, "Oh Gloria, don't be so serious, look at them, they only want to be friendly, they don't mean any harm."

The Italians moved to the bench on which the girls had been sitting and sat down themselves. They beckoned for Mary and Gloria to sit with them. One of the men finally spoke,

"Memento madam, memento!"

"I wonder if he's a singer too," said Mary, "he does have the big chest for it, doesn't he?"

"Mary, stop it, stop talking to him, you're only egging him on. Coom on luv, we best get home."

"Ahh," said the barrel chested Italian, "so you are Mary, I am Vitorrio!" and with that he started to sing a nursery rhyme, "Mary, Mary, where does your garden grow?" He sung the words carefully and slowly and yet with a lilt of melody which displayed, or rather betrayed his clear tenor voice, and when he had sung the line two or three times he spoke again. "You see I speak Eeenglish, finitissimo, yes?"

He playfully raised his right hand, putting his thumb to his middle finger to emphasise the 'finitissimo' of his English speaking ability, and he never stopped smiling.

Mary found this quite appealing and not at all dangerous, while Gloria on her part was not impressed, to say the least.

"Coom on Mary, they're the buggers who fought for Mussolini, you can't be friendly with them.

"They don't look so dangerous to me," said Mary."The master in school told us that the Italians didn't really want to fight us, and besides, they're helping us now, with the farming, they say. Come on Gloria, let's just sit for a bit. I like the sound of their language, it has words in it just like ours."

Mary took Gloria's hand and the two sat down again but Gloria made sure that she kept Mary's hand clasped in her own. Mary tried to make introductions by pointing at her companion and saying Gloria and then to herself as Mary.

"Aha! Maria," said one, "and Glorie!" Mary found their pronounciation both romantic and appealing. The two men introduced themselves, one as Vitorrio, which he Vitorrio pronounced with a flourish and the other man was Alberto.

"Oh, pleased to meet you Vitorrio and you Alberto," said Mary. "You see, Gloria they have names just like us, it sounds like Victor and Albert, doesn't it."

When the men heard this last comment, even though they could not understand it's meaning, they did recognise the English equivalent and it made them burst into laughter, saying, "No, No," and then pronouncing the names with their proper Italian inflection, "me Vittorio, and he Alberto!"

Mary adopted an apologetic tone when she repeated after him,the names Vittorio, and Alberto, which made Vittorio again sing his nursery rhyme, "Mary, Mary, where, where does your garden grow!" and Mary to say "sing Aida, Vittorio, sing Aida."

Vittorio took no further urging, he dropped to his knees and sang the plaintive love song from Aida to Mary. She was transported with emotion. She sat, her hands clasped through it all and then she bent and kissed him on the forehead tenderly.

Gloria still held Mary's hand tightly and even though she too was affected by the beauty of the song her inhibitions towards these foreigners would not let her unbend.

"Come Mary, we best be getting 'ome now," she said pulling on Mary's arm, and making her stand with her.

Alberto tried in vain to whisper "Memento," but she was having none of it, and Mary had to stand with her.

Vittorio said something to Mary about 'tomorrow' and looked toward his watch. Mary understood—and the next night's meeting was planned in that instant, for seven o'clock.

The men stood and watched as the girl's footsteps receded down the path towards the road. Mary at one point turned and looked toward them and Vittorio raised his arm in a salute, while Alberto stood disconsolately by. She could not resist waving herself, at which Gloria chided her. "Don't look back Mary, you'll only be encouraging them and we'll never be able to come back here without them following us."

Mary was silent, she could think of nothing else but that haunting melody of Aida, she longed to hear it again.

The following evening, Gloria knocked on the door of the Holdwell cottage, and when Mrs. Holdwell opened the door she was most surprised. "Why Gloria! I thought you were walking with Mary. Mary went for a walk right after supper. Didn't she call for you?"

Gloria at once guessed what had happened, "I must have missed her, Mrs. Holdwell, She must have taken the short cut to the road. I'll just follow her and I'm sure we'll meet. Thank you Mrs. Holdwell."

Gloria could not wait to get to the stile at the beginning of the bridle path. She made her way to the gates of the manor house but she could see no one and she feared going down the path by herself. She went back home, meaning to watch Mary's house from the front window.

That evening, at seven Mary had walked to the gates of the manor house by herself.

CHAPTER TWO

▼

TO RENDEZ-VOUS OR NOT

Mary had some misgivings about meeting Vittorio so soon again. She knew that Gloria would not approve and the two girls had always been guided by each other's inclinations, good or bad. In some ways she felt that she might be cheating on their friendship by meeting this foreign stranger so soon, but she told herself that he was most polite and much older and therefore would not be much interested in her anyway. He seemed to be so tender, just in the way he sung to her, and so well mannered. Probably he would not be there to meet her anyway.

But he was there, waiting for her. He had a broad smile on his face as she walked to him and he took her hand in his and held it for a minute just looking into her eyes. His own eyes seemed to be close to tears, so happy was he and she was suddenly so happy herself that she had come.

He looked down the path toward the wood and a knot of fear settled on her for a moment. What if this man should want to walk down the path with her? The bridle path was notorious as a tryst spot and she and Gloria had watched countless couples cavorting in the woods. She held his hand tightly and turned back to the roadway. He understood immediately and they began to walk away from the pathway and to the well travelled road. He gallantly conducted her to the path, walking on the road side himself to protect her.

As they quietly walked to the village, they passed many of Vittorio's compatriots, and the way that each one of them greeted Vittorio and politely doffed his cap to her actually made her feel proud to be with him.

He seemed anxious to try his new found English language ability with her, constantly naming various points of interest along the way. He took a great delight in the names of the public houses, names such as the Black Swan, and the Nag's Head.

"What is Black Swan?" he would say, and she would make the familiar beer drinking sign, as if a glass were raised to her lips saying "not me, Vittorio". Whenever they passed a public house Vittorio turned to Mary and in his limited English, asked, "Coffee Signora?" Mary, though she knew the publican would probably make them coffee, was wary of being seen in the company of a stranger in the local for she knew it would cause endless gossip. She therefore hurried on saying, "no coffee here Vittorio." Vittorio would look genuinely crestfallen and say, "Ah, but in Milan and in Florence, and in Rome," his voice rising,"there are lots of coffee houses. Some day, maybe I show you!"

He knew that he was not allowed to enter the Public Houses, and she was happy that they did not have to, on this their first evening together.

They turned and walked together back to the manor house gates, and she thanked him for their walk and he in turn said "I thank **you** very much, signora! Perhaps we can walk again, tomorrow!"

To which she replied, "Perhaps not tomorrow, Vittorio," and seeing the extreme disappointment in his eyes, she added, "but the day after tomorrow, I will be free."

"Ah, then Wednesday, it will be then, signora," he replied happily, "Perhaps we can take a much longer walk, I will have much rest and will be waiting so happily for you. I would like to sing for you again."

To the prisoner Vittorio, this evening had been somewhat of a triumph. The fact that he was only a prisoner of war, which meant that he had surrendered on the field of battle and that he had been an enemy of this country, and had to wear his Italian Army uniform at all times so that he could be clearly identified as such, made a social life all but impossible for him and his companions at the manor. His homeland, where brothels were common and more or less of a staple ingredient in the life of any virile Italian male, made this land seemed strangely innocent and unnaturally straight laced.

It reminded him of his own little village of Parma, where he knew every one and every one knew him. It was impossible to have any kind of assignation with a young lady there, for if he did, he would be obliged to marry and support the damsel for the rest of her natural life. And the consequences of him not acting honourably in this regard were first isolation, then disgrace, and finally even the wrath of the father, which could be considerable. The 'tortures of the damned' was more than likely a phrase invented for such an unfortunate lover who failed to live up to his obligations.

And what is more, if he had simply taken a young lady for a walk as he had done here, and his mother had seen him, or worse still one of his mother's friends had seen him, his future would have been practically sealed.

Here in England, on the other hand, he felt no such compunction about associating with members of the opposite sex. Here he was unknown and there was no chance whatsoever of the girl's father being able to mount a campaign of disgrace against him. His lowly status as a prisoner of war gave him anonymity, and although he would have to be careful, he could not be condemned for a liaison such as this.

There was the language barrier, and the stigma of being a one of the defeated enemy, but there was also the prospect of very congenial companionship with Mary, Maria, as she would be known in Parma and there was absolutely no chance of this becoming a responsibility that he would have to bear for the rest of his life. Granted, she was very young, just graduating from school in fact, young enough to be a virgin, he suspected. One thing worried him, she was a beautiful young girl and he would be despoiling her, if he carried this affair too far. He knew he could not suppress his basic emotions if ever he were to embark on a romantic affair with her.

Still, it would be so easy, he felt; she loved his singing, and the way she held onto his hand, it would be like picking beautiful flowers, if they were to be alone in the woods. She was so innocent and so young, and he would be able to teach her all the secrets, the beautiful secrets of love. Yes this was his chance at last, he would be able to show her his manhood, and teach her how an Italian man performs!!

And yet, would it be fair to take advantage of this innocent beautiful young girl? Did he care, after all, he had heard stories of the British and the Americans and what they were doing to the lovely Italian signoras, he would only be exacting some sort of revenge.

These were the conflicting thoughts which coursed through Vittorio's mind that night and all the next day. So tormented was he that he decided that he would not meet Mary this evening or any other evening. Yet at the appointed time, he found himself wandering back down to the large stone gates adorned by Lion's heads, the insignia of the Howard family, the owners of the Harrowdale manor house.

He had polished his boots to a fine sheen, tightened his belt to the last hole so as to draw in his tummy as much as he dared, and resolved that this time he would act his thirty five years of age. He would meet Mary, and he would tell her of the difference in their ages and he would announce, much as he liked her company, he found the temptation of being with her too great.

These fine resolutions dissolved the very second he saw Mary again.

This time her blonde hair was demurely fastened back with a sequined barrette which left a small knot of curls at her neck. making her appear more mature, and in Vittorio Babando's eyes, much more desirable.

He put out his hands to her and she grasped both of his in hers, and for a moment they stood gazing into each other's eyes. He had promised himself that he would tell her of his own doubts but the smile and the eager look of anticipation in her eyes melted his resolve.

This time, they turned directly for the path through the forest, taking them down into the valley to the little running stream. Young boys and girls were playing close to the stream, daring each other to jump across. Some made it easily while some of the smaller ones were getting quite soaked, which provoked much merriment and laughter. Vittorio and Mary stood watching for a few minutes, laughing with the children. When one little boy fell completely into the water, they helped him out and Mary scolded him, saying, "your mother will not like that, Johnny, best you get on home now!"

They walked on until they came to a small clearing by the side of the path which seemed to be guarded by a giant Oak tree. The tree had made the clearing really because nothing could grow amongst the acorns which covered the ground. "This is where Gloria and I often come," said Mary, and she ran off the path and around to the other side of the oak tree. Vittorio followed and found her standing close to the tree, almost enfolded by the huge trunk. She was standing quite still, her back to the tree, her eyes uplifted, looking upward through the branches. He came close to her and she did not move. He kissed her full on the lips and still she did not move. Finally, he kissed her again, and this time her arms enfolded him too. She fondled his hair and played with his ear as he kissed her and his tongue searched hers, and the thrills of it made her shudder.

"Oh Vittorio, Vittorio, we musn't," she whispered, and turned her head to avoid his lips. His hands were exploring her body and she pressed herself against him in spite of herself. He gently lifted her and knelt to the ground with her in his arms and they sat with their backs to the tree, embracing.

"Sing to me, Vittorio, please, sing to me," she begged. "What can I sing?" he asked. "Do you know Santa Lucia?"

"Of course, but that is a love song, Mary. In my country, only lovers sing it to each other."

"Then sing it to me, Vittorio!"

Mary lay with her head against the Oak tree as the strains of Santa Lucia seemed to envelope her there in the forest.

He sang the last chorus so softly and as he did so he bent to her and kissed her passionately on the lips while he fondled her breast through the folds of her blouse. Deftly, he unbuttoned the blouse and gently touched her breast, then bent to kiss. She felt a wonderful sense of delight that her body seemed to be able to excite him so.

But when he touched her leg and his fingers began to explore she felt a sudden fear and just at that moment, footsteps could be heard on the path behind the tree. She quickly sat up and rearranged her blouse and the moment was gone.

Vittorio's passion had not abated, though, and they lay close to each other behind the tree while the solitary hiker, a woman in her fifties so it seemed, went unconcernedly past. When all was quiet once more, he bent once more to kiss her and his hands began to explore her whole body. She felt such a rush of passion this time that she could not stop him, wanted him more than she had ever wanted anything in her life.

The momentary flash of pain and the blood were as nothing to the ecstasy of this her first love experience. She would look back on this day many times throughout her life and reflect on the significance of it.

He had not time even to think of using the condom which he had picked up in the hospital ward. "My God," he thought, "I've got her pregnant the very first time."

Mary could think of nothing else but the fact that she was in love. She wanted this man more than anything else in the whole world, she wanted him to be free to live with her. She could think of nothing else but him and the life she would live with him. When they walked back along the path, she did not even want him to leave her at the gate again. She wanted him to come home with her but he carefully explained that he would be arrested if he did not report back to the prison camp.

Mary sat on the stone bench at the gate to the Manor house and pulled him down to sit beside her. He tried to explain to her that she must get home and take a salt bath right away, but she was unafraid, even happy that she might have Vittorio's baby. "You must take me home with you to Italy," she told him.

For Vittorio this reaction was completely foreign. He had not loved anyone so young before. His lovers had been women of the world who had taken him not too seriously, in many cases, thanked him, and disappeared into the night again. This one was more than just possessive like his mother, she took it for granted that by this one act, he was hers forever. He was afraid and he had to get away and think things out for himself.

He looked at his watch, and the time showed half past seven. Frantically he showed her the time and whispered, "must be in camp tonight," he said, "big, big meeting. I am so, so sorry!"

Mary's face showed her disappointment but she bravely replied, "It is alright, Vittorio, it is alright. We can meet again tomorrow."

"Yes, tomorrow," said Vittorio, "I do not see how I will wait till tomorrow."

"Tomorrow will come, Vittorio, tomorrow will come, my love."

He rushed away from her and up to his room in the manor, hoping that he would not have to speak with any of his fellow prisoners, or worse to listen to the usual ribald comments about his so-called sexual prowess. He lay quite still on his bed, and would not talk to his comrades. Had he fallen in love and if he had, how was he to tell his mother? Surely this little sparrow of a girl would not love him. She was too young and he was so much older. Why she was probably not even a Catholic. What would his family say?

By the next day, he had begun to think that it had all been exaggerated out of proportion. She would not possibly have fallen in love with him so soon. But did he love her? He had to admit that he felt a certain attachment, no that would be too ordinary. he actually felt love for her. He would show her his love this time.

They met on the morrow, just as Mary had expected. They went back to the tree and in the quiet of the evening they made love together once more, and it became something which Mary could not have lived without. The evenings became idylls of wondrous love and on Sundays they started to meet in the afternoon. Mary saw no more of Gloria for their regular Sunday walks and Gloria instead took to calling on Mr. and Mrs. Holdwell on Sundays. George Holdwell worried for his daughter, and when he did catch a glimpse of his daughter's friend he worried even more because he could tell that this was a much older man.

CHAPTER THREE

▼

INTERVENTION

During the next few weeks, Mary's mother, Emma Holdwell, became concerned over her daughter's well being. Gloria, her lifelong school chum and best friend no longer came to the house. Mary no longer looked for Gloria for companionship, her sole interest was centred around the war prisoner's camp. When questioned, she professed an intense interest in the beautiful singing which could be heard from the prisoner's choir in the evening. To her mother, she finally admitted that one of the men had been very kind to her and that she had taken him on walks through the woods. But she became angry when her mother suggested that possibly she had become 'involved' with her foreign friend. George Holdwell could not bring himself to think of this possibility, could not believe that his young daughter could be capable of any such behavior. He dismissed the idea entirely and was more apt to accuse his wife of unnecessary meddling, than to admit that perhaps his daughter might be in trouble of any sort.

Eventually, even Gloria came to accept the friendship, even though she could not bring herself to talk to any of the Italian prisoners herself. She was content to remain on the sidelines, as it were, and to watch the romance between Vittorio and her best friend. She did think it singular that she was not invited to accompany Mary and her friend on their strolls through the woods. "Vittorio is so self conscious, because he cannot speak

English, Gloria. Perhaps when he becomes more fluent he will not mind you being along with us."

Gloria reluctantly left the two lovers alone and said nothing to either of the parents.

Vittorio's romance did not go unnoticed in the camp either. The ranking Italian officer a Major Boscolini, was somewhat unhappy with his Lieutenant Babando. He knew that a scandal would not sit well with the local people in Harrowdale, that his men could very easily lose the generous privileges and excellent accommodations which they had been accorded as agricultural labourers.

Babando was summoned to meet with his superior officer, one day, privately. "Vittorio," said Major Boscolini, "what is this romance I hear of, which involves you and one of the local signorinas, and a very young signorina at that!"

"It is nothing, Major, I assure you, it is nothing! She is a very lovely lady, and she insists herself that we go for walks in the woods together, alone."

"She does, does she Lieutenant, and you, of course never refuse?"

"I can hardly refuse, Major. She is a very persuasive lady, and to tell the truth, I believe she loves me very much."

"Oh so it has progressed that far, has it? And you have even made love to her, taken her to bed, have you?"

Vittorio was becoming more and more embarrassed. "Why yes Major, we have, sometimes."

"Well, if it has to come to that, I hope that you are prepared to promise to marry this lady, Vittorio. If not, this unfortunate affair could be the cause of severe restrictions being placed on all of us here at the manor. At the very least, I hope that you are taking proper precautions. As you know, condoms are available at the orderly desk, free of charge."

"I am aware of that, Major."

"Then you are using them, are you?"

"I hardly know what to say, Major. That is a very, very personal question."

"Nevertheless Lieutenant, it is necessary for the good of all of us, and my responsibility to my men that I ask it. You are warned, Lieutenant. She is a very young lady I am told. How young is she, do you know?"

"I believe that she is seventeen years, Major."

"Seventeen only? And how old might you be?"

"I am twenty five, Major."

"I am surprised that you, an officer, who should know better, should be taking advantage of one so young, Lieutenant." To emphasise his distaste, the Major turned his back to the Lieutenant, saying,"Dismissed."

Vittorio saluted the Major's retreating form, and left somewhat chastened. His responsibilities as an officer would never be over, he realized. And he would certainly be more careful when making love after this. The romance which had made him so happy only yesterday now seemed to pose a threat to both he and his men. How could he tell Mary that he could no longer see her? 7Could he himself face that possibility even?

Major Boscolini was suddenly presented with a solution to his dilemma, one that would, happily for him, stop this useless scandal. An American Army staff car, carrying six American officers drove through the gates and straight to the portico of the manor house. It was a long black shiny Buick, its sleek shape outlined in chrome, and news of its arrival caused excitement and rumors throughout the camp.

Many of the men wondered about the chances of being shipped to America for the rest of the war. Some even speculated on the possibility of the end of the war and their chances of going home.

The speculation escalated when Lieutenant Babando was summoned to the Major's room for a meeting, and further heightened when it was seen that sentries had been posted, American sentries in the hallway leading to the Major's room. Try as they might to get within hearing range, they found it impossible even to listen at the windows.

Inside, the Major was speaking to Vittorio. The American, who was of Italian descent was listening carefully. "You, Lieutenant, are to be given the chance to shorten our war by as much as a year. You should be proud of this opportunity."

"I am, Major," said Lieutenant Babando, "just tell me what I must do and I'll be glad to do it."

The American General spoke, "Lieutenant, the Germans have we know, stationed large quantities of ammunition in store houses throughout Italy. If we were to find these, we could blow them up and the whole German army would be helpless. But if we fail to find them, they can fight on for months and live off the land, and you well know what that means."

"Yes," said Vittorio, "my countrymen would starve to death while they eat." Saying this, Babando's face showed his dislike for the German troops. "How can I help, Major?

The American General spoke again. "Lieutenant, we will fly you to Naples and you will escape from us. You will join the Fascistis who are still fighting us and that way, you will find ammunition stores. You will be contacted by our agents and we will see that they are blown up behind the Germans."

"I would like to blow up those stores myself, General, I know where some of them exist in Milan, already."

"That will hardly be required Lieutenant, in fact it would be dangerous for you to do it and continue to be of service to us. No, we have Mafia contacts in Sicily who can arrange these accidents very nicely, once we find the dumps."

"Then I am to be a spy, a part of the underground, and after the war?"

"Oh, you will keep your rank in the army if you wish, you may even be a captain by the end of the war, but when the war is over, you will be a part of the liberating forces, a hero, I can assure you," said Major Boscolini.

Vittorio could not hide a smile. "Then you Major, are not a Fascist, I can see now."

"No I have never had a stomach for this war and I do not like Germans at all."

"I, too, Major. Now, General when do we commence?"

"Lieutenant, we commence now, at this very moment. This suitcase contains an American uniform. Please put it on and put your own in the suitcase. We will leave together, and you will put on these dark glasses to look like one of us when you get in the car. No one must know of this. You will be in Naples tomorrow."

"What of the men here? What will they be told? And what about my things here in my room? Who will look after them?" Vittorio was also thinking of Mary, but he dared not ask this too.

"Lieutenant, we will say that you have been taken to a secret location for interrogation. Your room here and your things must stay where they are as if you were expected back. You must contact no one, and your departure from here will be secret." said the General, "Please change your clothes now so we can begin our journey."

The General spoke Italian fluently, but Vittorio noted that his accent bore the unmistakable imprint of Sicily. He must have contacts within the Mafia, he thought.

The American had already assured himself privately that the men in this camp were from the Milan area, and that their conservative northern accent would enable them to operate behind the German lines.

The American uniform in the suitcase fitted Vittorio perfectly. He put on the dark glasses and the American soldiers surrounded him as he left the room carrying the suitcase just as they had closely escorted the man who had carried it in. No one at the camp was able to discern that when the Buick sped away, it contained not six, but seven soldiers with their General.

He was taken to the American Air base near Luton, in England to be briefed, then flown directly to Naples in Italy to the American army headquarters. He made no contact with his family at first, his letters, which had been mailed regularly through the Red Cross to his family in Parma suddenly stopped. He had disappeared from the face of the earth, literally.

In Rome the brave Lieutenant Babando, recently escaped from an American prisoner of war camp, let it be known that he was on his way to join a unit of the Fascists at the front at Cassino. Instead, he took the first train north to Parma, his home where he was joyfully welcomed home by his mother.

In the coffee houses of Parma where the local men gathered nightly to discuss the affairs of the world, and around the fountain in the town square, he asked many questions of these men. He quickly learned to distinguish the Fascist stalwarts from the supporters of the Communists. In his role as a Fascist hero, he was soon able to ingratiate himself with the Fascists telling them stories of his exploits in North Africa, where the Italian army had been overwhelmed by the forces of the United States, vastly superior forces far better equipped both in the air and on the ground.

Regrettably,he was not that far from the truth when he described how their German allies had monopolized all of the arms and even the shipping, leaving the Italians helpless. It was no wonder that whole regiments had been taken prisoner as his had been. He was able to convince the Fascist leaders that they must guard the ammunition and arms stores carefully, for they were to be the last defence if the Allied Armies advanced past Rome into Northern Italy.

The Fascist mayor took him in hand and drove him to Cremona and to Mantua one night to show him the secret stores. "We must make sure the Communists do not find them after the Germans leave," said the mayor.

Vittorio thought it ironic that this man, charged with the safety of his area, had already written the war off as a lost cause. He sternly reprimanded him, "Mayor, this war will be ours to win, because the allies cannot get as far as Rome even. See now, they cannot even get past the monastery at Cassino."

That night, in the tiny room in his mother's house where he had slept as a boy, he carefully diagrammed the location of the two large storage depots which he had discovered.

He told his mother that his leave was finished, and that he must get to Cassino where fighting men were desperately needed. The Mayor congratulated him for his resolve, imploring him to be careful for the sake of his poor mother. His widowed mother, Antonia Babando lived only for her son, Vittorio. Her husband had died fighting the Germans twenty seven years ago now.

"Vittorio, must you go back to Cassino," she cried, "surely you have done enough for the Fascists by now. What more can they want of you?"

Having just got her beloved son back, she was reluctant to see him leave her so soon again.

Vittorio dared not tell even his mother of his real purpose. The knowledge alone would be enough to condemn her. "I must see an important General in Rome," he replied, "then I will be back to see you, I promise."

He went to Rome, his precious information safely concealed in the lining of his uniform hat,to meet his contact at the Trevi fountain. He sat for four nights, watching and listening to the local women discussing their schemes to combat the scarcities of war. The men were few, except for the German soldiers, who were the only tourists here now. He had to smile at the stiffness of the Germans with their attempts at flirtation with the women. Good, carefree Italian men would be pinching a few bottoms by now! He drew from his inside pocket a well worn edition of the Fascist News. There was open defiance for the regime by this time, and even people seen reading the Fascist propaganda rags were suspect. He was subjected to all kinds of manifestations of disrespect. Cigarette butts were thrown at his feet, people spat in front of him, in spite of the uniform he wore. One man in particular, and swore at him loudly, standing directly in front of him. Vittorio could see by the bright smiling eyes that the man was faking anger. "That newspaper, is it not out of date?" said the stranger, in the unmistakable accent of a Sicilian.

"Yes, it might be, but I have been at the front and I am just catching up," said Vittorio, giving the agreed response he had memorised at the American base. The barest flick of an eyelid beckoned him to follow, and as the man hurried away, he sauntered off in the same direction.

He waited until the man was at least a block away and about to turn a corner. The man glanced back one last time and disappeared around the corner, as Vittorio rose to follow. He fought the instinct to hurry as he slowly made his way to the intersection. Puzzled, he pondered the four directions at the intersection and finally chose the one which had so many of the curbside restaurants jutting out into the street. He passed four more intersections before deciding that he had lost contact. He chose a table and sat down, wondering what or when his next contact would be shown to him. He had not long to wait.

The waitress came to take his order, but instead she whispered into his ear. "Your friend is waiting inside," she said.

He went inside the restaurant to find a table occupied by the same man who had spoken to him at the Trevi.

"How did you find me here?" he asked.

"I followed you," he answered, "did you not see me behind you?"

He signals for the waitress and red wine is brought to the table, a rough red wine, typical of Italy. Pasta is served and the stranger orders the meal. It is grilled ribs of beef, with a green salad. He asks for a Provolone, a side order of cheese, neatly wrapped in a muslin bag to go with the wine.

When the meal is finished, he leans forward and says, "should you have anything of importance for me you could wrap it into one of these table napkins and pass it to me."

Vittorio's hat has been tucked neatly into the epaulet of his uniform.

He takes it into his hand and quickly removes the maps from the inside, and places them in the folds of the napkin, then puts the napkin on the table where the stranger can reach it. The napkin is taken into the stranger's lap, and then carelessly left on the table, crumpled and obviously used.

The Sicilian stranger points to the crumpled napkin, suggesting that it be removed from the table. Vittorio takes it back into his lap and finds a note inside, which he puts into his pocket. The Sicilian smiles and they leave together. They embrace on the sidewalk as they say goodbye to each other.

When Vittorio reads the message passed to him he finds five American twenties neatly tucked inside, and a note which orders him to go to Milan and there to contact a judge of the high courts. He grimly realizes that even the highest of the bureaucracy has begun to plan for the end of the war.

The next morning's news is censored, but he finds references to communist uprisings in the North around Cremona and Mantua, but the details are not given. His train journey to Milan is delayed the next two mornings by the news of catastrophic explosions. He makes his way to Milan where he conta4cts his judge, and is told of these explosions which have occurred at Mantua and at Cremona. A communist cell has been identified as the cause of the sabotage, and at first Vittorio feels some relief that nothing is said of his visit to Parma. His mother is safe.

He is saddened when he hears of the execution by hanging of four jailed communists, enemies of the powerful Fascists. The munitions dumps have been destroyed, but blame for the incidents have been laid to the communists. The mafia in spite of the war are still powerful, they have not lost one iota of their control over the country. None of the guilt comes to them, nor is he himself under suspicion. He is free to roam Northern Italy helping the Americans to defeat the Germans but at what cost? The mafia are as powerful as ever. What will happen after this is all over. Who will deal with the mafia, he wonders?

CHAPTER FOUR

▼

FORLORN

The day after the American limousine left the compound Mary came to the manor house gates to wait for her Vittorio. Vittorio was not there to meet her, which she found odd, and when fifteen minutes had passed, she began to think that maybe he was sick, or worse still, he had been hurt. Her fears for him drove her to think of walking straight up to the portico of the manor house, and she did take a few steps through the gates in that direction when she saw Alberto standing in the roadway.

"Alberto," she cried, "how are you, Alberto?"

Alberto's command of English was still very limited. He turned at the sound of his name, but when he saw Mary, he turned quickly and went inside. Mary stood waiting, thinking with relief that he was calling for Vittorio to come out of the building. Mary chuckled to herself, thinking how she might scold him for his tardiness.

But when Alberto came out of the door once more, he had a man with him whom Mary had not met before. He wore the stripes of a sergeant, and he came directly down to her.

Mary took a step backwards, thinking that perhaps she was being evicted from the confines of the camp, but the sergeant called to her in English, "Hold on a minute, miss, you are in no danger, but I have some information for you,

"You speak English!" said Mary, surprised.

"Yes, ma'am, I do. Alberto has asked me to tell you about Vittorio. You were looking for Vittorio, were you not?"

"Yes I was, I hope he has not had an accident. Is he hurt?"

"No Ma'am, he has not been hurt. He was quite well when I saw him last. I believe that he has left us for a short time but he will be back, I think."

"Did he not leave a message for me? We were quite friends, you see. I thought that maybe he would have left a message."

"No, madam, I am sorry to say that there was no message. We do not even know where he has gone."

At this, Mary's face began to blanche and the tears came to her eyes. "What has happened to him?" she asked, her voice on the verge of breaking.

"Madam," said the sergeant, "I am sure he is safe, I can tell you nothing more but our commanding officer wishes to talk to you, please, do not be afraid. Come with me."

Meekly, she followed him all the way to the manor house, oblivious to the stares of the prisoners loitering along the pathway. She was ushered into a sparsely furnished office behind which sat an Italian officer.

"Good evening, Signora," said the officer, "I am Major Boscolini, senior officer here at the camp. May I be of assistance to you in any way?" Mary was put at ease by the friendly manner, and by the care with which the Major pronounced each English word.

"I am so sorry to be a nuisance to you, Major," said Mary, which only made the Major spread his hands in a self deprecating gesture. putting her at ease. "I was looking for my friend Vittorio, Vittorio Babando, Lieutenant Babando. Do you know what has happened to him? Will he be coming back, do you know?"

"Signora, I can tell you that he has been transferred. I cannot tell you where he has gone. He has not been punished or disciplined in any way, and I can assure you that he was unharmed and in the best of spirits when he left this camp. I also know that he is a capable man, a brave man, and that he knows how to look after himself. I would even say that he will come back to you when his work is finished. That is all I can say at the moment. I am sorry signora."

Mary walked slowly home, her eyes downcast, scarcely able to keep her composure. She resolved to keep a vigil for her Vittorio, no matter how long it had to be.

Weeks passed, and she could no longer face the sympathetic stares of the prisoners in the compound. She abandoned her visits to the manor house gates, but now a new fear began to overtake her, she had missed her period again.

She had just turned eighteen on the day she and her mother Emma Holdwell had a tearful heart to heart talk together. "What will we do?" said Emma, "Mary, what will everyone think of you? Oh, Mary how could you do this to us?"

"I'll have to get rid of it," said Mary, "I'll just have to get rid of it, that's all."

"How long have you gone on like this," asked her mother, "I hope you haven't let it go on for long."

"It's been three months, Mother."

"Oh, my dear, that's too long, it could be dangerous if you tried to get rid of it now, dear."

"What can I do, Mother?"

"We'll see what your father says tonight when he gets home." When George Holdwell heard the terrible news he was devastated and astonished that his daughter could have got into such awful trouble. He would not countenance an abortion, however because he loved his daughter too much to risk her life so heartlessly. "You can go to visit my brother in Bournemouth," he said, "and no one will know the difference. You will have to miss a year at school though, and you can put the baby up for adoption."

"She can go to the hospice for Unmarried Mothers in York, can't she," said Emma, "no one need know and we can visit her there."

"That's a good idea," said George, "you'll have company, there."

"What company!" exclaimed Emma, "all those lost girls." "Now, Emma, don't take on so," said George.

Mary settled in at the hospice, and the Holdwells let it be known that she had gone to Bournemouth to live with her uncle, where she would be taking a course in dress design.

Her interests had always been along that line, anyway. She was further inspired by the necessity of making a maternity gown for herself and she was able to use the sewing machine in the linen room to alter some of her old dresses. When the girls in her ward saw what she could do, they begged her to help them, and, before long, she found herself so busy sewing that she forgot her own troubles.

Emma and George Holdwell visited her every week bringing news of the local folk at Harrowdale, but the news which she really wanted, word from the prison camp that Vittorio had come back did not come.

Her father visited the commandant to explain her concerns, but Major Boscolini could not give him any comfort. The major was sympathetic but he was unable to divulge anything beyond the fact that the Lieutenant had been transferred to some unspecified location.

George Holdwell tried to convince Mary to forget about him but Mary had a determined streak and she resolved to find the father of her baby. She talked constantly of the baby and her determination to keep her little love child and would no longer talk of putting it up for adoption.

"Do you mean to say that you are going to bring the baby home?" asked her mother, "whatever will people say!"

"I don't care what they say," Mary replied, "I've seen so many lovely babies born here and I want to take mine home with me. I couldn't bear to leave him for someone else."

George and Mary talked of this far into the night, and finally George came up with a solution. "We can tell people that you have fallen in love with one of those Canadian airmen. Let's make him a bomber pilot who is lost over Germany one night. He might have been an Italian from Canada. They have lots in Canada, too."

This seemed very logical to Mary, after all her Vittorio was in the forces and it would all seem logical. She could still wait for Vittorio, and her mother and father would be happy.

Mary's baby boy was born at the hospice and when she saw him, she was more determined than ever to keep him with her. She volunteered to stay on and do sewing for the girls on the wards while she was nursing her new-born son, and the hospice was only too happy to have her do so. She became expert at adjusting dresses to meet the needs of maternity, and her satisfied and happy customers in the hospice made her all the more confident that she could succeed as a dressmaker. Already she was thinking of herself as a family of two and of how she would achieve independence.

George and Emma came to York at least once a week during the time of her confinement. They were forced to admit to themselves that they were happy to see their new grandson.

Victor was a happy baby, he had his mother's disposition, but Mary could picture his father in him, with his round face, his black hair, and his long Roman nose. Emma especially loved him in spite of all the heartache his coming had cost them. George too was proud to have a grandson, and was full of ideas as to how he would be able to take him on walks around Harrowdale.

Mary and the baby moved out of the hospice to an apartment in York, where she could set up her dressmaking business for the patients. George and Emma came up to York just as often, for they now admitted to one and all the existence of their grandchild. The people of Harrowdale were told of Mary's marriage to a Canadian and of his sudden death on a bombing mission.Mary picked out a name from the Canadian casualty lists for her husband, and came home to a tearful reunion with Gloria and with her parents. She was now known as Mary Morden, the widow of Flight Lieutenant Morden, a bomber pilot of the RCAF.

She was disappointed to discover that the prison camp at the Howard's manor house had been closed when she returned to Harrowdale, and the prisoners sent home. She took young Victor on a long walk one day to show him the tree in the woods where he had been created. They were able to lie together in the shade of the knurled old oak tree She sang all she could remember of Santa Lucia to him, while she rocked him back and forth. "Oh, wouldn't your father have loved to see you," she whispered, He doesn't even know you're with me, poor man, oh, I do hope he is safe." A little tear coursed down her cheek and she made no attempt to wipe it away.

"Look at your ear lobe darling, it's just like your father's." She gently stroked the baby's ear marvelling at the shape of it.The actual lobe was missing and the ear seemed tightly attached to the head, making the ears appear smaller than normal. She remembered that Vittorio's ears seemed to be the same.

She spent many more weekends at home with her mother and father. George and Emma were only too happy to sit at home with their new grandson so that Mary and Gloria could meet again. Gloria could not help but notice that the baby bore an uncanny resemblance to the Italian Vittorio. She recognised Vittorio's black curly hair and straight aquiline nose at once, and Mary soon saw that she did. Mary admitted to Gloria that he was in fact the father and Gloria promised that she would say nothing. "You are the only one who suspects that my husband was not a Canadian," said she. She said nothing about his ears to Gloria, that would be her own secret.

Her dressmaking business expanded as the war finally came to an end. Her specialty of maternity designs became very popular as the veterans returned and married, and she soon had to hire assistants to help her, both in the showroom and in her sewing room.

She opened her first branch of the "For Mothers" chain in the large industrial town of Leeds. It was a good move because she could commute from Harrowdale quite easily. She still kept her apartment in York but she was able to leave young Victor with his grand mother when she went to work and while this was not too pleasing to Victor at first, be soon got used to it. She found an abandoned uniform factory in that city complete with design studios and cutting room. Her most successful designs now began to be mass produced, and she enlisted her father's help in doing the necessary accounting work.

By now, she needed more retail outlets for her small factory, and she picked Harrogate for her next "For Mothers" shop. Harrogate proved the most successful of her branches, but now with three widely separated shops it became more and more difficult to keep control. She decided to sell the retail part of the business and concentrate on the manufacturing sector. She contacted Marks and Spencer and many of the other large department stores showing them samples of her dresses. The response was so fantastic that she sold out of the retail end immediately, and with the money so generated she expanded and modernised her factory in Leeds.

Mary Morden's success story in post war Britain attracted much unsolicited praise from newspaper fashion columns and in various women's magazines, and her reputation spread to the continent. She received a letter from a man in Italy one day which intrigued her. This man told her of the opportunities in the Italian clothing industry, and of the new line of materials with innovative designs to which he had access. He also mentioned the advantages of opening a factory in Italy where she would be protected from the numbing effect of the trade union movement in the industrial heartland of his country.

None of these arguments swayed her, except the fact that this man was writing to her from Italy. She decided to take Victor and herself on a holiday to Rome. He was hardly old enough to understand the significance of this journey but she bought a folding go-cart for him, and a sturdy harness which she vowed she would never relinquish and set off. She kept the man's letter in her business case for this was the only ostensible reason for her journey, but she really had her own personal reasons for coming to this country.

From the first day, she knew that it had been a mistake to bring Victor. When she attempted to walk the streets of Rome, her expensive clothes and shoes, as well as the English manufactured go-cart and the well dressed youngster., marked her as one of the wealthy elite. She had only walked a few yards from the marquee of the hotel when a small boy of about ten jostled her from behind and pulled her purse from her grasp. She screamed in protest, "Come back here thief!", but she was unable to chase the young rapscallion with Victor in the go-cart.

An alert young passerby was able to catch the boy and make him give up the purse. He brought it back to Mary with a smile, saying some unintelligible Italian words which obviously referred to the young boys as pigs of the lowest order. Mary thanked him in English, which surprised the young Italian greatly, for he had thought her one of the wealthy Italian class and possibly the wife of some important government official. Surprisingly he was not too happy that she turned out to be a foreigner from England. "Hah! Eeenglish!" he exclaimed in disgust, throwing the bag at her feet when she tried to express her thanks to him. "your 'usban! Not here?" He seemed to be chiding her for going out without her husband, especially with a little boy in a carriage.

She, having come this far safely, did not want to admit to this stranger that she was alone with the baby. "He is busy," said she indignantly, "am I not safe on the streets with my baby?"

"But of course, signora, with bambino, yes, of course, but with your purse and without your husband, our children are thieves on the streets, do you not know that?"

"How was I to know that?"

"Hah! Ask your husban', of course, stupido!" and he walked away as if in disgust.

She gathered Victor into her arms folded the go-cart and hurried back to her hotel. She would find a taxi and be driven from now on. Victor started to cry as she lifted him, more out of fright at the harsh words spoken by the stranger than by the thieves who had tried to steal his mother's purse. She decided that she would forgo the sightseeing until she knew more of the Italian scene.

In her hotel room she phoned the man in Sorrento who had written her about her factory. The man, Guisseppe Alano, was extremely pleased to hear from her and insisted that he personally come to Rome to see her. He arrived the very next day having driven most of the night in his Lamborgini sports car.

He was waiting for her in the lobby of the hotel, dressed in a tan slacks and matching silk shirt carefully unbuttoned at the neck and long sleeves with pearl buttoned cuffs. He looked slightly tired from the effects of his long drive,but cheerful enough. He was not tall, Mary noticed, hardly more than five foot six, and not as well built as she remembered Vittorio.

"And now signora, we will forget about business for today because it will be my utmost pleasure to show you our beautiful Roma! You have a most beautiful son and he will come with us, of course."

"Of course," thought she, "you didn't think I would leave him in the hotel room alone, not a chance."

As if he had read her thoughts, he next asked, "Is it possible that you came to Roma yourself? Your husban', is he—?"

"I do not have a husband," she said matter of factly, "I am a widow."

"Oh that is so sad," he replied, "and you are so young and so beautiful. I am so sorry."

Mary blushed slightly, "Why thank you Mr. er, Signor Alano, there is no need to be sorry. I have lost my husband a long time ago, in the war."

Victor had been dutifully holding to his mother's hand up to this point, but he suddenly spied a water fountain in the centre of the rotunda. He freed himself from his mother's grasp and ran towards the fountain. Mary called angrily to him, "Victor, come back here," but he paid no heed. He ran to the fountain and stood happily splashing his hands in the water, reaching for the coins on the bottom.

Mary ran after her son, intending to discipline him, but when she saw him playing so happily she could not find it in her heart. She bent and carefully dried the cuffs on his shirt with her handkerchief. Alano came over, bent down smiling and said, "Now, leetle man, we'll find a beeg fountain for you to play in," then, turning to Mary, "I will have to show you the famous Trevi fountain where everybody comes for good luck while in Roma."

"But Signor Alano, surely you did not have time to waste on such trivial things," said Mary, "you must be such a busy man."

"Aha, I thought so too, but to take such a beautiful little boy and his even more beautiful mother to the Trevi! It will be an honor, which I will never refuse! Please, my car is waiting!"

Mary held her breath in astonishment when she saw the shining Red Lamborgini at the curb in front of the hotel. A touch of the key and gull wing doors opened. Mary watched as Signor Alano gently lifted Victor to the small jump seat in the back and carefully strapped him in. Then he motioned for the front seat for herself and adjusted it for her. She felt absolutely luxurious as she settled in and he expertly guided the Lam' into the traffic.

CHAPTER FIVE

▼

SORRENTO

The drive to the Trevi Fountain, through the streets of Rome proved to be an exciting one, to say the least. Mary was used to the steady disciplined tactics of drivers in England, where all traffic laws were meticulously obeyed, but this journey, at breakneck speed was nerve shattering. Alano cut across lines of traffic and drove perilously close to pedestrians who ignored the traffic lights as they wended their way from sidewalk to sidewalk on the narrow streets. She tried her best to remain calm but found herself cringing in her seat as Guiseppe narrowly missed sideswiping first a woman with a baby carriage and then came close to having a head on collision with a taxi which suddenly turned left in front of them at an intersection. She looked back at Victor to make sure that he was safely fastened still. He was being thrust from side to side in his seat belt, but at least he was smiling and enjoying the jostling. She cinched up the buckle on her own seat.

Alano was calmly smiling, even laughing as he passed close to the oncoming traffic, plainly enjoying the wild ride. "Aha, but you have to get used to the driving in Italy," he said, as he braked and sounded his horn simultaneously and pedestrians scurried from his path, "we drive on the right in Italy, and you drive on the left in England, don't you, Signora Morden."

Signora Morden thought that this had nothing to do with her nervousness whatsoever, but she politely had to admit that she guessed this was so.

"Do you drive in England?" he asked.

"Yes, I have just bought a Morris," she replied, "it is not so expensive a car as this, but it gets me around."

"I'm afraid that I could not drive a Morris in Italy," said Alano. "Here you must be able to, how do you say it, accelerato? go quickly from a stop, or the pestas will get ahead of me."

Mary took the pestas to mean the little two wheel low slung motor driven cycles which crowded every street. Their tiny motors hardly seemed capable of starting the vehicle from a standing stop, in fact she noticed that the drivers invariably started their cycles by pedalling. She surmised that Guiseppe's conception of the speed and power of her Morris must be low indeed.

She stretched her legs to brace herself against the firewall at the front of her seat, pressing the toes of her high heeled shoes to the wall. Her skirt was quite short, and the pressure of her feet against the floor made it ride almost to her thighs. Alano could not resist an admiring glance at her silk clad ankles and calfs, nor could he help remarking that, "you have a most beautiful figure too, Signora."

Mary was terrified to see that the light they were approaching was turning red and the car in front was applying brakes. She put her hands to the dash, saying, "red light, Signor, red light!"

The signor took his eyes away from the view below the dash just in time, came to a screeching stop, and looked most penitential, saying, "I'm so sorry Signora, please forgive me, I was, how should I say it, entranced."

Mary gazed at him puzzled for a moment but he gently laid his hand on her knee, saying, "yes signora, entranced."

She couldn't help a blush as she just as gently brushed his hand away, but she had to admit to herself that it was pleasing.

Around the next corner, he said, "here we are, the Piazza Trevi." They drove into a square, and came to a stop. Ahead was the curving stone steps leading to the ancient Trevi statue, surrounded by the famous fountain, bubbling water into the pool. "It is said that a coin dropped into this fountain will guarantee a long life, filled with love and happiness," said Guiseppe Alamo.

He parked on the edge of the piazza and they walked to the stone steps to sit beside the fountain. Mary gave Victor a coin to throw into the fountain but instead he tried to put it into his mouth. Mary hastily took it from him and threw it herself and Victor watched as it sank to the bottom. Victor contented himself with playing at the bottom of the steps, and Mary and Signor Alano watched.

"Ah, Roma," said Guiseppe, "so full of happy people. It is a pity that they are not all content."

"What do you mean, Signor Alano? Why are they not content? There must be work for everyone now. Look at all the young people with their Pestas."

"Yes, yes, here in the north, everyone is busy. There are factories, and there are offices of the government, but there is always the politics, the communists say "strike" and the people strike and the whole country strikes and the government resigns, and without a government, where is law and order? Now in the south, there are no government offices and no industry, and no communists either because the mafia are in charge. They protect us against the communists, for a price, the price of protection."

"But you said in your letter to me that Sorrento was a wonderful place to open my business."

"Ah, yes Sorrento! It is a beautiful city, cooled by the ocean breezes where everyone can work for himself or herself, where no one pays for protection because we have an honest mayor and an honest chief of police and where the tourists come to visit all the year round. A most beautiful city, the jewel of the Tyrrhenian Sea!"

"And the people are not so poor in Sorrento?"

"No no, in Sorrento we have the tourists who come and stay with us for the winter, many from England, too. And there are many skilled seamstresses in Sorrento. You can have a dress made overnight in Sorrento, and if you pay cash, it is cheap."

"And so you think that I should consider Sorrento for my Italian factory, do you, why not Naples? It seems to be a bigger city and it's quite close."

Mary thought of Naples as a large city like Leeds where she had been able to establish her successful factory.

"I am sorry to say that Naples was spoiled by the war," said Guiseppe. It is in the hands of the Mafia and it has been abandoned by the government, I think. It is not safe in Naples."

"The mafia," said Mary, showing alarm. "I thought the mafia was a thing of the past.

"No, it is stronger than ever now because they helped the Americans during the war. They blew up ammunition dumps behind the lines for the Americans and now they are claiming that they got rid of Mussolini for us. They want credit for everything so that they can run their protection rackets again.

"Why doesn't the government stop them then. Are they powerless?"

"Politics, that's what it is in Italy at the moment. It is our biggest industry. Between the Communists and the Democrats fighting for power and both of them fighting the Mafia and at the same time dealing with the Mafia! It is impossible!" Guiseppe's scowl turned suddenly to a smile almost of resignation, "so we Italians talk of love, Signora, and what about you?

Do you have a husband? You have a fine little boy there."

"I lost my husband during the war, as a matter of fact," said Mary, "he was a flier in the Canadian Air Force, he was shot down."

"The Canadian Air Force?" said Alano, smiling, "What town did he come from in Canada. I know many Canadians from the war."

Mary felt a sense of panic for a moment, as she tried to remember the name of any town in Canada. "He came from Toronto, I think, we did not have much time to talk about his country. He was killed when we were only married for a week."

Guiseppe wanted to communicate his sorrow, yet he felt so much better that this fine lady was not married, after all. "Signora, I wish to express my sorrow for you, and I am truly sorry that you lost your husband so quickly. I know how you feel because I have lost my wife in the war also.

It is a long story, however so we will change the subject and rejoice in this beautiful day, shall we?"

Mary could not bring herself to tell the signor the truth about her marriage, that it was only a ruse to protect her self at home. She had carried it so far by now that it would be impossible tell the truth, unless she could somehow find Vittorio, and show him his fine son. Signor Alano seemed sincere enough, maybe she could take him into her confidence some day.

"Your little boy is getting tired of playing in the fountain, Signora. Shall we get in the Lamb. once more so that I can show you the view from the Tivoli and there is a lovely family restaurante up there which we call

the Castle. We can eat outside on the patio. I'm sure that your little boy
would like it up there."

Mary and Victor did enjoy their meal of exquisitely cooked brook
trout and Victor especially enjoyed the roaming accordion players who
sang just for him. Young Victor fell asleep on the way back to their hotel.
Guiseppe carried him to the room and Mary carefully laid him on her bed
and covered him. She asked Guiseppe to have a drink of red wine with her
and he was delighted to accept.

"Thank you for the beautiful day, Signor Alano," she said, "I must say,
I hardly know how to thank you Signor."

"It is not thanks I want Signora, but first may I be so bold as to call
you by your real name? This is so formal don't you think?

Please, signora, what is your real name?"

Mary felt startled for a moment. Did he not believe that she was
married? But he could not know anything, and she calmed herself. "Why
yes, I was thinking the same," she said, my name is Mary, Mary Morden."

"Maria! as we say in Italy. It is a beautiful name for a beautiful lady,
My name is Guiseppe, Mary, but I should tell you that my Canadian
friends in the war used to call me Juice, for short, they said, so I became
known as the Juice!" he smiled.

"Juice!" said Mary, "I like it, Juice, do you like it?"

"Oh yes, I like it, you can call me that if you like, because you are
partly Canadian, aren't you?"

Mary winced inside a little but she admitted to her split nationality
this one time. All in good time, she would be able to set things straight.
"I think you had better go now, then Juice, because I am a little bit tired."

"Yes, of course," said Alano, "tomorrow is another day and I must show
you the Roman ruins the Forum and the Colosseum, that is fabulous."

"That would be wonderful," said Mary, getting up from the sofa and
extending her hand to Alano. He tenderly held her hand until they came
to the door, and she stood close to him. He put his hands on her shoulders.

"Thank you for a wonderful day, Juice," she said softly.

"The pleasure has been all mine," he replied, as he bent and kissed
her forehead.

The next day Alano took Mary and Victor to see the famous Colosseum
and the ancient Roman forum and ate lunch together in St. Peter's square.

"Thank you once again, Juice, but I need a rest from this heat, I think
Victor and I would like to go back to our room for a rest.

Do you mind?"

"No of course not," said Alano, "perhaps we can meet for supper?"

"I would like that, but this time, it is my treat. We will have supper at my hotel."

"There is no need for that Mary, after all."

"You have been marvellous,Guiseppe, simply marvellous.

And now I would like to make some small gesture. Could you come to our room at five tonight?"

"Yes, I will Mary, thank you."

Mary and Victor took their much needed rest and Mary arranged with the lobby to have their dinner served in the room. This would save her any embarrassment over the meal check.

They would be able to talk of their business plans also but Mary had many questions to ask of him first. She had no doubt that she could easily fall in love with this country, its climate and its ambience, but she did want to know how dangerous it really was, for one thing. "I certainly like the name these Canadians gave you, Juice," said Mary.

"Many of them have asked me to come to Canada," said Alano but I can't leave my Italy, my family is here.

"Tell me about your family, Juice," asked Mary.

"I just have my mother and my sisters now, my sisters help me in the leather factory. We make shoes and belts, mostly. We have about twenty people working for us."

"And did you say that you lost your wife during the war?"

"Yes I will never forgive the Germans for that, she was taken as a hostage. I never saw her again."

"Why was she taken?"

"It was because of me, I was helping the Canadian soldiers who were caught at Salerno to escape from the Germans. Many of them stayed with us until the Germans found out. Then I had to hide because the penalty for helping an allied prisoner was death. They couldn't find me so they took my uh, uh" tears began to form on Guiseppe's face and Mary put her hand in his, "my wife."

"That's terrible," said Mary. "I hope it doesn't hurt you to be called Juice then, does it remind you of it too much?"

"No, it's quite all right, Mary, especially coming from you, since you were also bereaved."

Mary winced again. She bit her lip and was silent for a moment, which Guiseppe took to mean that she too was remembering.

"When you come to Sorrento I want you to meet my mother and my sisters, Mary. I know they will like you, and I hope you will like them."

"I want to see Sorrento, it sounds like it would be the ideal place for my European factory, I would have to find a supplier for material."

"I can help you there, too. Our home seamstresses import cotton from Greece and the colours and fabrics are excellent."

In Sorrento, a partnership was formed, and Mary and Guiseppe became the owners of the "For Mother's" factory in Italy, which produced the light cotton dress lines to complement the linen and wools made in England.

Mary rented a small one and a half bedroom apartment for herself and Victor. It stood on a high rise above the town of Sorrento, overlooking the Tyrrhenian Sea. The apartment was on the second floor of the building, above a leather shop, the type of shop which abounded in Sorrento, made its reputation in fact. Guiseppe had found the apartment for her, because of his business connections with the leather trade. He had purposely looked for one close to his mother's house in the piazza San Georgio. Mrs. Alano's large residence would easily have accomodated Mary and her son but her conscience would not have allowed Guiseppe to even suggest such a move.

Guiseppe's mother took an instant liking to Mary, even though there was an obvious language diference and, to her mind, an insurmountable religious conflict. She wished that her son could forget about his murdered wife and get married again. Mary's appearance was the exact opposite of his first love. Whereas his Italian wife had been dark complexioned with long flowing black hair, Mary was blonde with her hair trimmed short and her English rosy cheeked complexion seemed to radiate health and good cheer. Signora Alano begged Guiseppe to take Mary to church to meet the priest, but Mary carefully avoided any attachment. When the pressure became too great Mary would go back to England to see to her factories and business there, but she was drawn back to Sorrento because she loved the city and she found herself attracted to "Juice" her business associate.

Victor too took an instant liking to Sorrento. He picked up the language from the Alano family much faster than did Mary and took to staying with them when Mary had to leave on her business trips.

Her comfortably easy friendship with 'Juice' grew with their association together. Mary found it impossible to tell him of the real story of her marriage, and he in turn found it frustrating that she could not resign her self to a new love and a new relationship. Mrs. Alano was saddened by the turn of events, which made their friendship more akin to a brother and sister than to a love affair.

When Mary saw that 'Juice' was becoming friendly with an English tourist who made it her business to come to Sorrento more often than usual, she found herself almost overcome with jealousy. She asked Signora Anna Alano, Juice's mother to look after Victor one night. Mrs. Alano happily agreed to take him, for she saw the purpose in Mary's mood that day. Juice was just as happy to accept her invitation to a special supper in her apartment. She made him her favorite English supper of Yorkshire roast beef with pudding and even made a trifle for him. Then in the candlelight she served a bottle of Frascati red which she knew he loved.

When they sat on the sofa together, she told him that she might be ready for marriage 'again'. Juice took her into his arms and they kissed long and passionately. The wonderful feeling of a man's body close to hers that night released years of frustration with an outpouring of love and emotion which she had not experienced since that day under the oak tree in Yorkshire. Her love for her son Victor was unabated, but suddenly she had a new purpose in her life.

It was impoaaible, she could not go on like this. She would have to forget Vittorio once and for all. Juice was a wonderful caring man and she could hardly afford to wait any longer.

"Juice, I hope you don't mind, but I have to go to Florence next week."

"That's wonderful, we can go together," said Juice.

"No, please, I have to go by myself," said Mary, "I have written to this company and they have asked that I meet with their purchasing agent."

She made an appointment to see a Mr. Alfred Braschi, purchasing agent of the San Raphael Department Stores. In the executiveoffices of the firm in Florence, she noted the name of Mr. Braschi on the notice board but she also saw another name which brought back memories for her. A Mr. J Boscolini was listed as the Vice President of the firm. Could this be the J. Boscolini, who was the Major in charge of the prisoners in the Manor house in Harrowdale?

The secretary would probably know, she thought, she would ask if their Mr. Boscolini had ever been a prisoner of war in England. She must be careful in asking such a question, because she did not want to reveal herself, until she was sure. It might make it embarrassing to have it known that she knew one of the highly placed executives when she was supposed to be calling on one of the buyers.

Mary spoke to receptionist to ask if she might also see Mr. Boscolini for a moment. "Do you wish to see Mr. Boscolini now or later, Signora? Your Mr. Alfredo Braschi is ready to see you now."

"Oh by all means, I will see Signor Braschi now, Signora, May I see Signor Boscolini when Signor Braschi is finished with me?"

"May I make an appointment for you then? Who shall I say is calling?"

Mary hesitated again. How should she introduce her self? "Please say that it is Mary Morden uh, the former Mary Holdwell. He may not remember me, I am sorry to say. NO please don't say that! Please just say that we knew each other during the war and I would like to ask him something, uh, tell him something." She was becoming more flustered than ever, and to make matters worse, when she looked up at the receptionist, she could see that the girl behind the desk believed her to be some woman from Boscolini's past, exactly the impression she did not want to project. She made a rapid retreat to the buyer's office, her face flushed with anger at herself.

When her interview with the Signor Braschi was over she dreaded the walk through the reception office again, She was actually relieved to be told that Signor Boscolini had gone out of the office and would be unable to see her this time.

In fact Mr. Boscolini was only just now leaving the office. She watched him change his own in-out board marker and recognized him immediately. He seemed to look straight through her as he passed her on his way out.

Mary dared not speak, she was sure that the receptionist must have warned Signor Boscolini, of this woman who evidently wanted desperately to see him.

She would go back to Sorrento and write him a letter. He might be able to tell her something of Vittorio, even though now it did not seem to matter so much. But at least, for Victor's sake, it must.

CHAPTER SIX

▼

MARRIAGE AT LAST

Giuseppe's mother, when told of the impending marriage was quick to begin the preparations for the wedding. She hoped and prayed that Mary would consent to be married in Sorrento and into the Catholic Church.

Mary had only one nagging doubt. She loved Juice and he loved her and she couldn't stand the thought of losing him to that English tourist girl. Besides, they had a most profitable and pleasant business relationship together. Life with Giuseppe Alano would be so beautiful, so comfortable. They would go back to England for visits but their life would be lived in Sorrento with its wonderful views of the Amalfi Coast and the Isle of Capri, on the Bay of Naples.

But she had come to Italy to find Vittorio, her first real love, and Victor's father. She felt that she had a duty to find him to let him know that he had a son. If she married Juice, Giuseppe, now, would she be cheating herself and cheating Victor? It was only fair to Victor that she find his father and show him his son.

Seeing Major Boscolini in Florence reminded her, and renewed her determination to find him. He had not deserted her, after all, he was taken from her by the war and if she could only just talk to him, just once, she would be satisfied.

Strangely enough, that first night alone with Juice, when both had expressed a love for each other, had triggered enormous change in Mary's attitude. She had Juice, and she had her former life of which Juice knew nothing. Keeping these things bottled up inside of her, for she could tell no one in Italy, made her nervous, and edgy, positively cranky, even with Victor. She found herself constantly embroiled in pointless arguments with her employees and Giuseppe had to be summoned almost every day to break some kind of an impasse. Juice would manage to settle her down but even he would be accused of disloyalty, for taking sides against her.

He recognized that she was distraught and tried to calm her fears with protestations of his deepest love, but when even this made no difference, he asked her to go to England to see her parents with him. She however, insisted that she go alone with Victor first so that she could tell her parents, and he was left with no alternative but to agree. He promised that he would follow her in a week, so that he could meet her family, as she had met his.

Once back in England, and freed from the obligations of the Alano family she recovered from her nervous disorder quickly and soon immersed herself in the operation of her English factory. She was able to talk to her father about Vittorio and to ask him what she should do.

"My darling, you have grown so much and accomplished so much. I hardly know what to say to you. Of course I am pleased that you have come to ask my opinion, honored even, but if you feel an obligation for Victor's sake, then by all means try and find Vittorio." He was silent for a moment, then he asked,"couldn't this Giuseppe be a father to Victor too?"

"Yes father, but he is not really his father. I want him to know his real father as I know you. Don't you think it would be right that way?

"Does Giuseppe know of this?" her father asked.

"No, he does not. I couldn't tell him, ever."

"Well, the first thing you might do is to write to this Major Boscolini from England. That would be a good starting point. But make sure and tell him why you want to locate Vittorio, that you have his son, and you want him to see his son."

Mary wrote the next day, using her letterhead from her Leeds factory to give herself further credibility.

It was a short clear letter, coming straight to the point.

June 11/49

Mary Morden, Managing Director,
For Mother's Clothing,
16 Lion's Head Road,
Leeds, 21, England.

Mr. J. Boscolini, Vice President,
San Raphael Department Stores, Inc.
25 Piazza Signoria,
Florence, Italy, 3245.

Dear Mr. Boscolini,
   I write today on an extremely personal matter, a matter of great importance to me.
   Some weeks ago when I visited your offices I recognized you from the time when you were in command of the prisoner of war camp near Harrowdale, Yorkshire. At that time I met and fell in love with Lieutenant Vittorio Babando. His son is now almost five years old and should see his father.
   Could you help me to find Victor's father?

Yours truly,
Mary (Holdwell) Morden

She wrote the letter herself painstakingly, in Italian, using an Italian English dictionary to assure herself of her spelling, wrote the words, 'Personal and Confidential' across the front of the envelope, and mailed it to Italy before Giuseppe arrived in Yorkshire.

Giuseppe arrived driving his prized Lamborghini auto, much to the delight of George Holdwell. George proudly introduced him at the Black Swan to his friends as Mary's Italian fiance. Juice found the bitter tasting of Yorkshire Beer much to his liking. He soon got over his initial shyness in the Black Swan snug room. Many of the locals had stories to tell of their associations with the Italian prisoners during the war.

He had to be especially careful with his driving, however, and he and Mary had many hair raising adventures together, particularly on the busy highway to Leeds. It was during one of their times together at the factory, that an answer to Mary's letter came in the mail. She hastily put the envelope in her purse, out of sight and retired to her private office to read it.

Juice had gone down to the factory floor to try and solve one of the problems in the cutting room.

Mary recognized the letterhead of the San Raphael department store immediately on the envelope. She noted with satisfaction that Mr.

Boscolini had marked his letter with Personal and Confidential caution, and his name appeared underneath the name of the store on the return address. She was hurriedly slit the envelope and unfolded the letter.

It was not a typed letter, it was the untidy handwriting of an executive not used to writing his own letters. Boscolini had penned it himself. It read;

My dear Mary Morden,

I have just read your letter and I am astonished, yes astonished, yes even stupido, that is how I feel that I did not remember you when you came to my office in Florence! If you had only told me that you were the Mary Holdwell who came to me in Harrowdale, looking for Lieutenant Babando!

Now before I say anything else, I must tell you how pleased we are to be selling your women's dress lines. They are most original and so liked by our customers! Thank you for showing us at San Raphael your latest products.

Now as to the whereabouts of your Lieutenant Babando, I can only give you this information. Lieutenant Babando was given his release from the prison camp to go back to Italy and to work for the Americans in secret work behind the German lines. That is why he could not write to you. He was ordered to work for the Americans to disrupt the German supply lines. I heard after the war that he was able to find many ammunition stores in Northern Italy, and that he supplied this information to the Americans who worked with the mafia to blow up several important storehouses and thus helped to defeat the Germans who were occupying our country.

Since the war, he has done much important work for the government in identifying the enemies of democracy in Italy and we who are veterans look to him as a hero. I can tell you no more except that he has been seen by some as being connected to the communists, and by some as moving with the mafia. But I fear I am telling too much and I must ask you tear this letter and burn it as soon as you have read it. If it should be traced to me, my life would be in danger. I can only say to you that I am certain he is living somewhere in Italy at this time. I know that his mother lived at one time in Parma. When you are next in Italy, and in Florence, I will be most pleased to see you.

Yours truly,
James Boscolini

Mary read and re-read the letter. She had been told many. things, but the things left unsaid were by far the most sinister. Vittorio had worked as an undercover agent in the part of Italy, occupied by the Germans, that was sure. His life was at risk just as Giuseppe's was. But since the war, Vittorio had continued his undercover work it seemed. Was he working for or against the Communists? What about the Mafia?

Vittorio must be considered a dangerous man by now, feared by even his former comrades. She would be putting her own life in danger to try to find him, and Victor's maybe. It was no use, she decided, she would put him out of her mind altogether. She would make a new life with Juice.

She would marry Giuseppe Alano, and live forever in her beloved Sorrento. That part of her life was gone forever. Giuseppe came back into her office from the cutting room floor, just as she was crumpling the letter. He stretched across the desk to kiss her but she drew back saying, "silly boy, you silly boy, close the door quickly dear, we do look foolish like this." He made a show of being disgusted, "these English, they think there is no love left in the world, but there is, my dear there is, and it's my love for you." He walked to the door and closed it carefully, before coming back to her again. This time he walked around the desk, gently lifted her to a sitting position atop the blotting pad, and with his hands placed provocatively on her upper legs proceeded to kiss her lips, her ear, and her neck.

"Oh Juice," said she, "I love you so, but we mustn't, not here." She had stuffed the crumpled letter into her purse, and she would burn it in the fireplace as soon as she got home.

George and Emma Holdwell were overjoyed to see their daughter so much in love, and making her wedding plans. Mary and Giuseppe made appointments with the Rector of St. Marks English church, and Gloria and she shopped for the wedding and bridesmaid gowns. Giuseppe went home to Sorrento to ask his mother's permission, as was the custom in his family. His mother, Antonia Alano wanted her son to marry at home and with a truly Catholic ceremony, but all her fears were quieted when her priest suggested that the service be conducted in Sorrento a second time. Giuseppe was dubious about broaching the subject to Mary but she was happy to oblige. "Won't it be wonderful, Juice? We'll have two weddings and two honeymoons! And on top of that, I'll be able to show my mother and dad our beautiful Sorrento.

Accordingly, an English wedding was held in Harrowdale at St.

Mark's parish church, and a proper English wedding feast was catered at the prestigious White Swan Hotel in nearby Bradford. Mary and Juice, with Victor safely strapped in the back seat spent the next two weeks on a driving honeymoon through Belgium France, and Switzerland and back to Sorrento. They were waiting at the Naples airport to greet George and Emma Holdwell and Gloria and her mother and father. Giuseppe had insisted that all five, who had witnessed the English wedding also be present at the Italian. He had paid for their passage, and they in turn were pleased at the opportunity to see Sorrento. George Holdwell jokingly said to Giuseppe "You must have made a pact with the almighty to arrange this beautiful weather Juice."

To which Juice replied "No pact signor, this is our weather, the kind we have all the time, except when the rains come, or Vesuvius decides to blow!"

But the rains did not come and Vesuvius remained calm and the Italian wedding went just as beautifully as Antonia had planned for it.

With the wedding over and the guests departed for England, even Antonia, Guiseppe's mother accepted that Guiseppe had become Juice, and Mary's affectionate nickname for him became his everyday name.

Mary and Juice settled into the villa owned by the Alanos. Giuseppe would gladly have supported his wife and adopted son on his considerable income from his leather business, but Mary hated to part with her companies, now that they were becoming most profitable. The For Mother's factories in Sorrento and Leeds became ever busier as the line became known throughout Europe, and Mary found herself travelling on promotional tours almost every week. Juice tried as much as possible to integrate his own travelling plans with those of his wife, but his leather business did not take him to the same type of retailer, obviously. Mary wanted to get in as many of these promotional trips as she could for she was sure that she would soon have to consider staying at home. She and Juice lived for the day when they could have a child together, and every month she prayed that she would conceive. Antonia even taught her to light a candle in the church but for month after month she was disappointed.

"I think we had better get away from each other for a good rest," said Mary one day, "I'm so sorry Juice, so sad and I want your baby so much."

"I know dear, I know, but where will you go? To England?"

She smiled and looked horrified at the thought, "Oh no dear, not that far and not that long, please. Would it be all right if I go to Rome with Victor for a few days, I want him to see the Vatican and maybe we'll even see the Pope!"

"I want to see some real Romans, daddy, with swords!" said Victor, "and lions and tigers, in the cowossm." He had been playing soldiers with his friends at the kindergarten and had heard the stories of the wild animals and the gladiators in the colosseum. His dad had made him a wooden 'Roman' sword which he proudly wore, tucked into his belt, when he went into the piazza to play.

"The Romans with swords aren't there any more," said Giuseppe, "but you carry your sword with you, just in case, eh!

You never know when you might need it."

Mary chided her husband, "Juice, stop filling him with nonsense like that, we'll have enough to carry without that sword." Turning to Victor she said more softly, "I'm afraid we won't have room to carry the sword, my dear. Look, it won't fit into our suitcase, even."

"All right, Mary," said Juice, "I'll make him a little leather belt with a scabbard so he'll be able to carry it with him all the time. Come with me Victor and we'll soon have this solved."

When Juice and Victor returned from the workshop downstairs, Victor proudly wore the sword at his waist, and to the delight of his father he would not allow it to be taken from him until he was tucked into his bed.

The next morning at the station, Giuseppe kissed them both goodbye, "You must wear that sword all the time now, Victor," and to Mary, "watch for the small boys around the Vatican, my dear." Giuseppe was referring to the small army of petty thieves which seemed to infest every corner of the Vatican complex in Rome.

Mary was glad that she had chosen public transportation. The bus was most comfortable, they soon came to know their fellow travellers, and the scenery was magnificent. She was glad that she had decided to go by bus rather than drive herself. They arrived in the Piazza della Minerva at their hotel, and that night she and Victor walked to the nearby Gelateria for a cup of Italian ices and sat contentedly watching the people in the piazza.

▼

CHAPTER SEVEN

A TUNE REMEMBERED

The next morning she lay in bed and watched Victor playing in the room with his sword. Victor imagined himself in historic Rome because he could see the famous monument to the emperor Hadrian in the distance. He was bravely marching into Rome at the head of his legions, sword brandished high, with his grandmother and grandfather Holdwell riding behind in chariots, having come all the way from Britain. She could not help but marvel at the way Juice had been able to fire his imagination with these stories from ancient Rome, not to mention the way Victor himself had interpreted these same stories and adapted them as his own. She lay quietly in the bed with her eyes carefully closed not daring to peek as Victor marched back and forth across the room.

Suddenly, she could hear shouts and the sound of running from the street outside and she rose to investigate. Victor had heard it too and they both stood at the patio window which led to the balcony. Hordes of people were running towards the Piazza from every direction. They were gathering in the open square and one man was handing signs to those who would carry them. Her first instinct was to close the curtains and shut out all of this activity but she was too curious for that.

She threw open the patio door and she and Victor went out onto the balcony to watch. She knew what could happen if this were England. A

Bobby would come riding up and demand the permit for such a noisy assembly, and if it seemed to be a strike against coal mines for instance he would order the strikers off the street and back to their picket positions at the mines. But this was no mere miner's strike. By the signs and the slogans being shouted, this was a political gathering, and it looked to be a gathering of the Communists, of all things.

The Communists had elected many of their people to seats in the National Assembly lately and they were a force to be reckoned with now, instead of the mere rump party they had become in England. There was much good humour throughout the crowd as they arranged themselves in tidy cells behind the signs and it was evident that a parade was being organized. Several bands appeared, and Victor begged to go outside and watch. Mary and he stood in front of their hotel as the parade formed and began to wind its way around the huge Pantheon. building. Victor pulled his mother as they followed the parade along the Via della Minerva and into the Piazza Rotunda. He was enthraled with the drummers and the musicians shouted encouragement to him and his mother as they marched along. "Come with us to the Piazza Navona, we'll buy you an ice cream!" said one.

Mary laughed at the invitation, but she bravely walked along with Victor all the way to the Piazza Navona. The word Navona was taken from the ancient Roman words which described a race course and indeed it could have served as such today so large was this Piazza. Now it was virtually lined with gelateria, ice cream and confectionery shops.

As the procession entered the huge Piazza, a lone policeman interrupted the parade by riding into the square on horseback. He rode straight towards the largest signs being carried demanding a permit, for they could hear him say "Permesso" loudly. He was greeted with curses and catcalls; some even tried to pull him from his horse. Mary took refuge with Victor inside the nearest shop. Luckily for Victor, it was the famous Tre Scalini Cafe and of course he wanted an ice, she bought him the specialty of the house, a chocolate tartufo, and one for herself. It was delicious, she found. The demonstration in the Piazza became more and more boisterous so that Mary was glad to be inside and away from it all.

When the threats to his safety worsened, the mounted policeman blew his whistle and as if on cue, dozens of police poured into the square, armed with truncheons and what looked like grenade throwers. The grenade throwers were actually tear gas canisters, and the sight of this weapon instilled fear in some of the demonstrators, others objected strongly, became clearly angry.

The police moved forward quickly, and made several arrests. These unlucky ones were put in handcuffs and made to sit on the pavement of the Piazza to await the patrol wagons. Sensing that it was now safe, Mary brought Victor out into the Piazza just as the last patrol wagon drove into the square. Six men were being loaded into the back of the black wagon, and with a start, she realised that she knew one of them. He was much heavier now and he was unkempt and his hair was long and sloppy, but was it possible? She ran out into the street to get a closer look, and as she came close to the Black Maria she looked inside through the wire screen. He was sitting with his back to the wire and she was able to look at him from the back. His ears were quite small, they had no lobes! She called, "Vittorio, Vittorio," and he turned to look out at her, stared straight at her, a look of disbelief and astonishment on his face.

He was an obvious rabble rouser for the Communists, one of the ringleaders of the demonstration which was about to be staged in the Piazza. He called out sharply to the driver, "memento! memento!" but his captors took no notice. The driver seemed to want to drown out his cries as he raced the motor in lower gear so that it roared as he slowly made his way through the crowds of people and left the Piazza.

Mary suddenly remembered Victor back at the curb. She turned and ran back to find Victor frantically running this way and that in search of her. She knelt as they saw each other and he rushed into her arms. "Oh, Victor Victor, I just saw your daddy, your real daddy! I'm sure it's him, I'm sure."

Victor, puzzled, replied, "Daddy back home, mommy, daddy back home."

"Yes, dear, of course, daddy is back home, isn't he?" she said tenderly.

Vittorio had seen Mary, had looked upon the sight as an apparition come to haunt him from his past. This could not be, simply could not be, the English girl he had loved in Yorkshire. And yet, the accent was English, he could not doubt that, and the same blonde hair with the same page boy curls. How could it be anyone else?

His fellow prisoners in the van could see that he was becoming very agitated and tried to calm him, "It's all right Vittorio," said one, "we had five thousand out there today, we'll have fifty thousand next week and nothing will stop us. Did you see how stupidly the police were acting?

They wouldn't even let us march today. The people will know how they stopped us. They'll read it in the paper. Democracy, freedom, Pah!"

But their remarks only seemed to enrage Vittorio. He pulled at his handcuffs desperately, swore at the driver repeatedly, "stupido! stupido!, bastardo!" until finally the guard sitting opposite hit him solidly on the mouth, breaking the skin of his lips. When they finally arrived at the station house his manner became more objectionable than ever. He wrestled with the police until the Sergeant shouted, "one more word and it's the 'hole' for you Vittorio!"

Vittorio knew that his lips were bleeding and he lurched toward the Sergeant rubbing his bloody face on the clean uniform. "It's the hole for you, then Vittorio, two weeks in the hole for sure!"

Vittorio was taken away, literally thrown inside the elevator which was to take him away down into the ancient Roman dungeon, now used as a place of solitary confinement for the unruly prisoners. The guard brandished his night stick saying, "don't try anything in here now I warn you, you won't get out alive!"

The elevator jerked to its resting place on the dungeon floor and the guard motioned for Vittorio to follow him. They walked a short way down the damp corridor to reach a small room which was sparsely furnished with a single desk on one side and a bench on the other facing. A sergeant approached from the other end of the corridor to stand behind the desk. "Only one more this time, guard?"

"Only this one, sergeant."

"Right, dismissed," and the guard took the elevator back up. Vittorio, his hands still cuffed, awkwardly reached into his breast pocket and withdrew his identification from a secret compartment, saying, "you seem loyal and honest enough. I'm looking for an honest man!"

A look of great relief showed on the sergeant's face as he recognized the code, "I thought for a minute your cover must have been blown. By the look of your face, you made your point this time Major."

Vittorio held the rank of Major in his country's security forces. He was known to the outside world as a worker for the Communists who had been imprisoned many times. He was really a State Security officer working in the secret intelligence branch of the Italian Police. His secret mission was to find and identify the dangerous people within the Communists, the people who were actively planning the overthrow of the government.

Now, he wanted only to come out of this disguise and get back to the Piazza Navona. He had to be careful that he did not reveal himself to his fellow prisoners in the van, nor to the police arresting officers. His position was an extremely dangerous one, that of infiltrator within the Communist political party.

He had joined the party and enthusiastically taken part in countless demonstrations against the government, been arrested and imprisoned for his activities, and in jail had so irritated his captors that he had been put in solitary confinement in the 'hole', many times. Within the party, he was admired for his dedication to the principles of the 'revolution', the so-called final solution when International Communism would engulf the world.

The sergeant in charge of the 'hole' was really a Captain in the security forces and the only officer in the station who knew him for what he really was.

No one in the party had yet realized that his solitary confinement in the dungeons was really the escape avenue he used to return to his real life world. His phrase of "looking for an honest man" was instantly recognised by the sergeant. His handcuffs were removed, and he quickly took the security elevator to the fifth floor of the station. He had ripped away his unkempt wig disguise before the door opened to his office.

"Major Babando, are you hurt? Your lips seem to be bleeding," said his secretary.

"Nothing, nothing, my dear. Have my car brought to the front door would you please, Andrea?"

He raced down the four flights to the street level to await his automobile, and was blocks away from the station when he remembered that he still was wearing his disguise clothes. If he should ever be caught or seen by a member of his cell he would be instantly recognised and unmasked as an infiltrator. He picked a quiet section of town and changed to a sports shirt and light coloured gabardines from the back seat. Quickly he brushed his hair and used his electric shaver to remove the three day stubble he had accumulated. He arrived at the Piazza Navona less than three hours after he had left it so ignominiously that morning.

He knew that he would look conspicuous sitting in his sleek Alfa Romeo but he felt that the disguise he had effected earlier would shield him, and he would not be again recognised as the rabble rouser of the Communists. He was right, nobody connected him with the mornings disturbances, but neither could he find what he was looking for, the disturbing image of his past life, the English lady. He drove slowly around the whole perimeter of the Piazza, stopped in front of the magnificent Fountain of the Four Rivers to watch the tourists come and go, but he could recognize no one.

He drove back to his office thinking perhaps that his imagination had got the better of him. The excitement of the hour, and the turmoil within him had affected his judgment. He would soon have to give up this double life, much as he relished the challenge, and much as he felt it his duty to rid the country of the Communist threat. He had been too long in the struggle, ever since he had been enlisted in the battle to eject the Germans.

He had been recruited by the right wing parties to help in the fight against the Communists because of his war time connections with the Mafia. There was a corrupt part of the right wing which leaned to the Mafia for protection, and he tried to distance himself from this group. Really, he felt a certain kinship with the struggles of the working men in the factories, who were the core of the Communist party. He longed to get out of politics once and for all, but he realized that he knew too much now.

Should he ever be exposed as a member of the elite police he knew that the Commies would have a price on his head, and similarly if he told one half of what he knew of the protection paid by the right wing industrialists to the Mafia to secure labour peace he would be shot.

Mary Morden Alano was assailed with thoughts about her life too, after this encounter in the Piazza. Should she try to contact this man who so closely resembled Vittorio? What if it should not be him and she made a fool of herself? On the other hand, if it was him, and he still loved her, what would she be able to tell him, that she was already married? She owed all of her love to Guiseppe really, on the other hand Victor should know his own father, shouldn't he?

Why oh, why had she consented to the wedding so quickly, when she had promised herself that she would wait forever for Vittorio. If only her life could be backed up like a movie reel, and she could play this part again.

In the end she decided to find out once and for all if this had been Vittorio she had seen. She found some pamphlets lying on the pavement after the police had left the Piazza and took them to their hotel. There were addresses and phone numbers for the local Communist party offices and she went to her room and started phoning. She asked for Vittorio

Babando but was told that names could not be given over the phone, she would have to attend at the offices personally. She did however note that the name was not unfamiliar to the party, and she was heartened, at least. Victor was hungry by this time, he wanted to go to the gelateria for ices. Mother and son came down from their room together and made their way back to the Piazza Navona. It was just at that moment a sleek Alfa Romeo drove out of the square. The convertible top was down and there was something familiar about the driver. He too looked like Vittorio from a distance. Now she was thoroughly confused. It seemed that every second man she looked at looked like Vittorio. She wiped her forehead with her handkerchief and rubbed her eyes. Did she have some kind of fixation about him?

When the waiter came to serve them at their table, she decided to at least make some inquiries. "Could you tell me anything about where those people who were arrested this morning could have been taken?" she asked.

"Probably to the station on the Piazza Stazione," replied the waiter. "If madame would like a taxi to go there, my brother will drive you. Do you wish me to phone him?"

"I must get there quickly," said Mary, "will your brother come right away?"

"But of course, senora, he is always quick," said the waiter.

The waiter promised he would phone and Mary sat down to wait. She waited fully forty minutes, during which time she saw several taxis cruising around the Piazza, and she was in bad temper when the waiter's brother finally drove up.

The waiter swore mightily at his brother Antonio for being so late, but he only smiled in reply and indicated to the waiter, his brother, that he had to have his siesta, after all. Mary wondered if all this anger on the part of her waiter was really just to impress her.

At any rate, they arrived at the Piazza Stazione in only five minutes and Mary realised that she could have made it on foot in much less than the forty minutes it had taken for the taxi to arrive at the ristorante.

"I insist on waiting for you, senora. There will be no charge for the waiting, I promise you," said her driver Antonio. Mary rushed into the police station holding tightly to Victor's hand as she did so. She asked for a man named Vittorio who had been arrested that morning, but she was only greeted with suspicious stares from all the officers in the station. When many of them edged closer to the desk and became interested in her plight, she had the feeling that they wanted to find out if she knew something incriminating about this man. Questions were directed at the desk sergeant and re-directed to her such as "How friendly were you with this man?" and "Did this man harm you?" and even

"did he steal something from you?"

Mary kept her temper at first and answered the questions with a direct "No, of course not." but she worried that she might get herself in trouble with these police officers if she did not give any more valid reasons for her search. "I believe he is the same man I knew during the war," she admitted, "we were friends in England."

"Aha," said the sergeant, "so it might have been an affair of the heart." It was clear that many of the other officers in the station had come to the same conclusion. Their snide smirks as they edged away from the desk revealed their feelings.

Mary was outraged at this invasion of her privacy and her tightly closed lips showed it. She stood staring into the sergeant's eyes as he looked straight at her. Even the officers who had been watching the exchange turned away in embarrassment. Neither spoke for almost 15 seconds but finally the sergeant averted his gaze and looked straight down at the papers on his desk. "I am sorry madam, I know of no one here by the name of Vittorio.

Does he not have another name?", "Yes," she said, "of course he did. His name was Babando, Vittorio Babando. Now for the last time, can you tell me if he is held here."

The sergeant consulted his papers once more, and this time he was all smiles. "We have a Vittorio Babando here, it seems. He was arrested only this morning,but already he has been such a trial to us that we have had to put him into solitary confinement."

"What does that mean?" she asked.

"It means madam that he cannot see anyone until he is released from the dung-, pardon me, from solitary confinement. It means that he must be held for two weeks and he is not allowed visitors."

The sergeant could see that tears were showing on her cheeks and that this was no matter to take so lightly. "What can I do, I must see him," said Mary plaintively.

"I am so sorry, senora," said he. "Perhaps you would like to leave your address, maybe he will write to you."

Mary hastily scribbled her hotel's address and phone number onto her own business card "for Mothers" and left it with the Sergeant.

The desk sergeant was unaware of Vittorio's real status at the station. His real identity was a closely guarded secret known only to the sergeant in the basement and the state security offices on the fifth floor, which were out of bounds to all police personnel. The only clue to the real Vittorio was the x which always preceded his convict number. To the police, it meant that he was a serious violator, and that any and all communications to him or from him must be reported to the fifth floor, that it was a matter of state security.

Thus it was that, as Mary again left the stazione in her taxi an Alfa Romeo was being parked underground, and Mary's card, and Major Vittorio Babando arrived on the fifth floor together.

"A lady was downstairs just this minute asking for you," said Andrea, his secretary.

Vittorio hastily picked up the card, read the name Mary Morden Alano, and the business name For Mother's in relative calm. The name Mary had alerted him somewhat, and the Italian surname left him completely in the dark, but the handwritten (Holdwell), below the Italian Alano was a lightning bolt to his conciousness. He immediately returned to his car and drove at top speed to the Piazza della Minerva.

In front of the hotel he parked and was about to get out of his car when Mary's taxi pulled up. Mary and her young son got out and hurried inside before he could speak to her. Mary merely glanced at the Alfa Romeo, took no notice of its occupant, being engrossed with her own problems and those of Vittorio in solitary confinement. She took Victor by the hand and hurried with him to her room.

For his part Vittorio wanted a private meeting himself, one that would not reveal his identity in public. His position as a Major in the security service was an extremely sensitive one. There was one other point too and a very important one. This Mary Holdwell was married, evidently to an Italian, and a mother. He showed his state security pass to the man at the hotel desk and discreetly asked for the room number of Senora Alano. He went to the house phone and dialled her number. When she answered, he said "Hello Mary, it's Vittorio."

How could these saucy taxi drivers have discovered that she was looking for Vittorio, thought Mary. She must have let it slip somehow. and she would have to be more careful.

She said angrily, "I don't know where you get your information, you fellows, but I am not interested and I have found Vittorio, thank you."

She was about to hang down the receiver when the voice on the other end said, "No, no, I really am Vittorio, Mary Holdwell, I have your card, with me, your For Mother's card."

"Where are you?" she said.

"In the lobby, Mary, do you remember Santa Lucia?" and he sung the first few bars. "Can I come up to see you, Mary? please."

CHAPTER EIGHT

▼

DISCOVERY

"Vittorio, is it really you? So that WAS you in the paddy wagon. But I thought that you were arrested, what happened? And where is that ugly long hair? It made you look so fierce this morning! Have you escaped? The police told me that you were to be locked in a cell for the next two weeks. I had given up the thought of seeing you."

Mary could hardly believe her eyes when she opened the door to her suite. This was not the man she had seen in the paddy wagon, this was much more like her Vittorio, the man she had last seen on the Howard estate in Harrowdale, in Yorkshire.

"Things are not what they seem in Italy these days, Mary. You must never tell anyone that you saw me like this. We are in a life and death struggle for a decent Italy." Vittorio took her hands in his and held her at arms length, "my beautiful English Mary, Maria, what sweet memories this brings to my heart."

"Come sit down, Vittorio. You really are very gallant to call me beautiful now. We've all been through so much over these years, haven't we?"

"But you are beautiful, Mary, more beautiful than ever. The years have made you blossom like a rose."

"And you still have the gift with the ladies, Vittorio," she smiled, raising her finger in embarrassment.

Vittorio was sorely tempted to take her into his arms and hold her close to him. Only the presence of the little boy Victor in the room held him back.

"What have you been doing all these years, my darling? What is this 'For Mothers'? Is it a nursing home or something?"

"No silly, I have a factory now and we make maternity clothes for mothers, and since the end of the war, we are doing very well, thank you. Now what about you, Vittorio? I still haven't forgiven you for leaving me so suddenly, I missed you so much when you left Yorkshire. You can't imagine how badly I felt, Vittorio."

"Mary, my dear I missed you too, but my orders were secret and I couldn't tell a soul, not even my own mother, bless her immortal soul. I always hoped that some day I would find a way to come back to you."

"But you never did Vittorio, and now it seems I have come back to you. We both have so much to tell each other, but let us forget the past, it's gone and forgotten. Tell me about yourself now, Vittorio. What are you doing now?"

"My dear Mary, how hard it must have been for you to understand."

"Yes, but I had a letter from Major Boscolini just last month, telling me about you, how you had done so many important things to hasten the end of the war in Italy"

"Major Boscolini, I wonder how he knows those things. I haven't heard from him since the war. What has he told you about me? Those things are best forgotten anyway. Please tell me about yourself, Mary."

"First you must meet my son, Victor Vittorio. Here Victor, come and meet my friend Vittorio."

"He's a fine boy, Mary. Aren't you Victor? Oh I see you have brought you Roman sword with you. May I see it?"

Victor showed his sword proudly to Vittorio. "Now that's a fine sword," said Vittorio, brandishing it in the air and making professional cutting strokes. Where did you get such a fine sword?"

"My daddy made it for me," said Victor eagerly.

Vittorio looked to Mary, and she could tell the disappointment in his face. "Ah, your daddy," he said, "and where is your Daddy now?"

"Sorrento," said Victor, "we are going to see Daddy tomor row, aren't we, mommy"

"Maybe, Victor, maybe," said Mary.

"He's a fine boy, Mary, how old is he?"

"He'll be turning six in January Vittorio. He was born in January of 1945, you see."

Quickly. Vittorio recalled that he had been in Yorkshire in May of 1944, and the significance of it dawned on him.

Mary appeared not to notice saying, "come here Victor, I want Vittorio to see something." She gently turned his head so that his ears were plainly visible to Vittorio and he saw that they were without lobes just like his own.

Vittorio stared at the ear lobes, put his fingers to his own, then as he looked at Victor's jet black hair and his sturdy build he came to the realization that he was looking at his own flesh and blood. He looked once more to Mary, "Why didn't I know?" he whispered.

"How could I tell you," answered Mary." I was all alone. There was no one I could talk to except my own mother and father. I went to a nursing home and had him, and nobody except Mother and Father and Gloria know who the father is. Everybody else thinks that I married a Canadian who was killed in a bomber raid, and that my husband's name was Morden.

I started making maternity dresses for the patients in the nursing home and then branched out to my own stores and now I have two factories, one in England and one in Sorrento. I am very successful Vittorio!"

"And are you married?"

"Yes, I am married to a wonderful man, Guiseppe Alano, and he is Victor's father now."

"And you love him?"

"Yes I do, of course I do."

"But you still wanted to see me didn't you. Why Mary?"

"Because you are Victor's father. And I had to ask you Vittorio, why you did not come back to me. You promised to come back and you never did."

"My darling, there is nothing I would rather have done than come back to you, but my work here is so secret that even my family cannot be told. I could be shot if I were found out. Some day I promise you, when Italy is safe, I will be able to get out of this but right now I must be silent."

"Why do you stay in this work then?" Mary asked puzzled.

"I am working in the secret service, Mary, I cannot get out of it. If I tried, the Communists would want me killed to protect their secrets, and if I told what I know about the Social Democrats, I would have the Mafia down my throat. It is a vicious circle and I just have to hope that I am doing this for Italy's sake."

"Have you been in this work since the war?"

"Ever since, yes, ever since the war, there has been no respite. We had only just got rid of the Krauts when the Commies wanted to take over. Italy has had a hard and difficult time. But tell me about yourself Mary, and how has this fine son been, eh? Vittorio picked up Victor and held him on his knee. "You are a fine strong boy, your mother has looked after you, my boy. How do you like Rome eh?"

"I like Tartufos," said Victor. "Mommy, can I have a Tartufo, please may I?"

"You had a wonderful Tartufo, just this afternoon, Victor, and now it's almost bedtime. You can have one tomorrow, I promise," said Mary.

"Will you read me a story in bed, Mommy please."

"Yes dear I will, I have wonderful story about Toto the elephant." Mary took her son into the bedroom and put him to bed. He was so tired from the day's activities that it took but a couple of minutes of the story reading and hardly a page turned before Victor fell asleep. She gently closed the door and came back out to sit with Vittorio.

Vittorio longed to reach out to her, to envelop her in his arms. Instead he put his hands in her lap and knelt in front of her. "We are two lovers who will never again see each other, probably," said he, "but I would like to do something for Victor, he is my son after all."

"What would you like to do?"

"I want him to attend the best schools, in England I think. Can we send him to Eton?"

Mary laughed. "Eton, that would be practically impossible, Vittorio. In the first place, young men must be born into the aristocracy to attend Eton!"

"We will solve that easily. Do you know that there are certain places at Eton which are reserved for foreign students? My connections with State Security will allow me to enroll my son in Eton. The English would gladly do that for the Security office, I know. We supply them with valuable information about the Commies all the time, and they know that."

"And how would I tell my husband about this. He thinks that Victor is the son of a Canadian bomber pilot."

"That is so easy Mary. I will call at the department of Industry and Commerce and have them sponsor your son to Eton. It will be a gesture of appreciation for your factory in Sorrento."

Mary was amazed. "You will be able to arrange all that!"

"We are the State Security Service, Mary, and nothing is more important than the security of the country. Nothing is impossible for the State Security Office."

She put her hand over his on her lap and pressed down, "that would be wonderful, if you could do it, Vittorio."

"But Mary, I must see him often, I have only just met him, and already I love him like a son. He is a sweet boy, isn't he."

She bent and kissed his head, cradled his face in her hands, "Vittorio, Vittorio, I knew it would be like this. What are we to do?"

"It will help if I can see the boy often Mary. I want to see him grow up. The rest will be our secret."

"How can we keep all this a secret? It would be impossible."

"Impossible? Hardly," said Vittorio. "I have been living a double life like this for years. Some people think that I am a rabble rousing Communist, constantly being jailed, while others know me for what I am, a Major in the Security Service. It will be easy. We will just tell your husband that I am a friend of Major Boscolini whom you first met a the prison camp in England. I will come to Sorrento on business and we will meet. Now where will we meet? At your house if you wish, yes I think it better if we meet at your house, so that I can bring Victor a present when I come."

"Oh Vittorio, he will be spoiled rotten with two daddies looking after him.

"And he'll deserve it because he has such a fine and beautiful mother," said Vittorio.

To which Mary added, "and a handsome father too eh." She winked at him as she said this, and put her arms around his neck.

Emotions built to a peak as they held each other, kissed ever more passionately, until Mary whispered, "Oh Victor, it's wicked, we shouldn't, should we?"

But hands gently caressing bodies only fueled an uncontrollable passion within, and when they finally laid back, exhausted, and Mary began to collect her clothes strewn on the carpet, she whispered, "Oh Vittorio, what are we to do?"

"Mary, my sweet Mary, I will always be yours, I knew that some day, we would be together again."

"No, Vittorio, it must not be like this. How can I love a husband and you too?"

Victor woke at this point, and began to feel lonely in his strange bed. He called "Mommy, Mommy, I want you, Mommy."

"I have to go into him now, Vittorio, I think you had better leave, don't you?"

"Yes I guess it is best that I do. Give my love to my son, won't you dear. My son, just think, my own son! I'll phone you in the morning, Mary dear."

When he had left, Mary quietly slipped into bed with a comforting whisper to her son, "Here I am Victor darling, here I am.

Did you enjoy your day in Rome today?"

Sleepily, he said, "Yes Mommy, I like the parade and the Tartufo. When can I have another Tartufo?"

"Tomorrow dear, when it is bright and sunny again, we'll have another one, but now we must both get to sleep."

Victor soon dropped off to sleep again, but Mary laid awake until dawn. When at last she saw the first hours of sunrise she became drowsy enough to sleep herself, but she awoke every few minutes as her thoughts wandered between Victor, Vittorio, and Juice, her husband.

Vittorio quietly left the hotel and drove towards the Piazza Navona. His large Alfa Romeo would cause some to turn and stare, he knew, but now, and for the first time since the war, he didn't care. Up to now he had been very circumspect, lest some one with sharp eyes and a good memory recognize the poor communist in the obviously well-to-do man in the Alfa Romeo. He drove slowly, wondering which shop Mary and Victor had entered to buy their Tartufos He hardly noticed the couple lurking in the shadows who seemed to be looking for something on the sidewalk.

The man suddenly straightened and looked in Vittorio's direction, "Vittorio, Vittorio, what are you doing here?"

Vittorio, in the Alfa Romeo, suddenly interrupted from his reverie, knew he had been recognized by one of the members of his communist cell. In his anger at being caught so easily, he depressed both the clutch and the accelerator, bringing the motor roaring to life. This focussed attention to him and caused many more people to stare in his direction. He raced out of the square with gears clashing and tires screaming.

The stranger on the sidewalk had been looking for a watch that he had lost in the melee after the parade that morning. He exclaimed to his companion, "How could that be? That was 'Lobes' Babando, I'm sure of it. I saw his ears even, and if that was him, it solves a problem."

"I know what you're thinking Titus, but that couldn't be. It can't be Vittorio, didn't you see how the guards roughed him up this morning? They wouldn't rough up one of their own like that."

"Nothing but a scratched lip, and besides, even his own guards might not have known, if he's part of State Security."

"Not Lobes, he's a loyal worker, and a hard worker, he hardly ever misses a demonstration or a parade, or even a meeting. Except when he is in jail."

"Haven't you noticed how the police seem to be ready with tear gas when we want to mount a real demonstration? How do you think they get to know where we are to meet? You don't tell them do you? No and I'm sure I don't. There's got to be an informer somewhere, and maybe we've found out where."

"God if he's really part of Security and we know about it and he knows we know, we could be in trouble ourselves. Do you realize that? What can we do, Titus?"

"We'll watch him, that's what. Say nothing to anybody for now but watch him, take a close look at what he does when we plan our next demonstration."

"We could go to the Stazione and make sure that he's in the dungeon. That way we'll know if it was him in the Alfa."

"To much of a risk, because then he'll know that we know he's an informer and both our lives would be in danger. It's not worth it. Let's go home and say nothing."

Titus and his girl friend went home and tried to forget the incident. In the meantime Vittorio 'Lobes' Babando had rushed to the Stazione himself in his Alfa Romeo, intent on repairing the damage to his 'cover'.

Vittorio parked underneath the building and hurried to his office in the Security section on the top floor. He went by elevator from there to his dungeon cell beneath the building, determined to establish credibility for what he had in mind. He knew that Titus had seen him and that he faced an almost impossible task of convincing him otherwise.

When Titus and Juanita arrived home that evening, their phone was ringing, in fact had been ringing for the last half hour, so that even the neighbors could hear. When Titus answered "Allo" the voice on the other end gave a sigh of relief which could be heard over the line clearly, "OOOH OOH, am I glad you are home Titus," said the voice, "I've been calling for most of the evening, hoping you would come home."

"Who is this?" Titus asked.

"It's Lobes, Titus. I need your help, they've been beating me up here. Please, can you get me a lawyer, fast!" Vittorio hung up the phone with a resounding clash, leaving Titus with no time to reply, as if his guards had suddenly interrupted him.

Titus turned to his girl friend Juanita, genuinely relieved saying, and "I guess maybe that wasn't Lobes we saw in the Piazza Navona after all He's still in solitary and they're beating up on him, he said. He wants us to get a lawyer for him right away. I'll phone the Police and make sure he's there.

At the Police Stazione Vittorio had already spoken to the Desk Sergeant ordering him from the Security Department to relay any calls that came in regarding the prisoner downstairs to them. He identified himself only as the Security Officer on duty.

Five minutes later, the phone rang, and he carefully placed a piece of tissue paper over a comb to disguise his voice when he answered it. The caller was in fact Titus, inquiring about the prisoner in solitary. He assured Titus that Vittorio Babando was being held under the tightest security and could not be contacted under any circumstances.

It was close call and he would have to be more careful in the future.

CHAPTER NINE

▼

HOME FROM HOLIDAYS

Mary lay in her bed after Vittorio had left the suite, full of apprehension, and wondering literally where to turn next. She had married Juice because she had given up the idea of ever seeing Vittorio again. The marriage had been solemnized by both their churches and in front of their family and friends in England as well as in Italy. It was a firm union.

What had she done to this marriage by her infidelity with Vittorio on this night? Would 'Juice' forgive her if he knew? She doubted it. She would have disgraced him in front of all of his friends, and that was unforgivable. Also the story of her first marriage would be proven false, and she would be labeled a loose woman not fit to be part of the Alano family. Her factory might even suffer, for she would never again be able to count on the Alano family for help.

She began to curse the fate which had brought her to this hotel in Rome at just this time. She should never have allowed Vittorio to come back into her life, and she never would have, she told herself, if it hadn't been for Victor, she wanted him to know her real father. But that was wrong too she admitted. It wasn't that she wanted Victor to know his father so much as she wanted Vittorio to see his son.

It was good that Vittorio was a man with influence in the Security Service, enough influence to have Victor enrolled in such a school as Eton.

That would be wonderful, but again she began to have doubts. How could she explain this to 'Juice', and to the Alanos.

She slept only fitfully that night, she was constantly awakened by her dreams, first by visions of Vittorio laying beside her, and then tormented by scenes of Guiseppe pointing an accusing finger at her. She was awakened early by a telephone call from the front desk. A messenger wished to deliver a letter for her hand only. She quickly put on a dressing gown and went to the door to receive the letter, half expecting that Vittorio would be delivering it himself.

It was an officer from the Security Office who insisted that she reveal her maiden name, before he would release the letter. She gave it 'Holdwell' and he handed her the letter and left. The letter was from Vittorio. It read:

My Dearest Mary,

It pains me to write this letter because you may think I have 'disappeared once more.
The truth is that as a loyal comrade in the party, I must not be seen in public for at least three weeks, for fear that my work in State Security may be endangered. I will not be able to see you for now in Rome but I will come to your home in Sorrento. Please don't worry, I will be most discreet and I will not give our secrets away.
Ever more yours, Vittorio.

P. S. Please my dear, tear up this letter and burn it as soon as you have read it. VB

There was no fireplace in the room and she did not have a match so she crumpled the letter and pushed it to the bottom of her purse. She would not see him anymore in Rome this week. It was a relief at least not to have to battle with her conscience again.

For two days more she stayed in Rome taking Victor to the fabulous gardens and water falls of Villa d'Est in Tivoli. On their last night, they walked to the Piazza Navona for a chocolate Tartufo. Then, at dusk they sat watching the young men on their little motor cycles come into the Piazza for a cappuccino. It was almost eight o'clock before they walked back to their hotel in the Piazza Minerva and Victor was well and truly tired. He dropped off to sleep as soon as he laid down, but Mary slept only fitfully.

What was it she wanted? What was best for her and for Victor?

'Juice' and his mother were waiting at the Stazione to greet them the next morning in Sorrento. "You didn't stay too long in Rome" said Mrs. Alano with a smile. "Could it be that you wanted to get home to Guiseppe? I know I used to be happy to come home to my Titus after such a trip."

Mary hoped that her somewhat guilty smile would be taken by her mother in law as a gesture of endearing embarrassment.

Victor too, was happy to arrive home, happy to greet his daddy once more and to tell him about the things he had seen in Rome. Guiseppe listened enthusiastically to all that the boy had to tell him. He somehow felt that if he could not depend upon the devotion of Victor's mother at all times, he might earn it by his love for her son. Mrs. Alano was overjoyed to have her family back together in Sorrento. She embraced Mary as the newest member of the Alano family, and even Victor who, despite being Mary's Canadian son seemed to be growing up to be a healthy Italian boy.

Mary seemed happy enough with her married life, although to Guiseppe, it appeared that something might have come between them. This went on for some weeks, during which Mary, although outwardly happy, became inwardly concerned over the visit which she knew would come at some time from Vittorio and even a mite fearful of the consequences.

Mary and "Juice' were sitting together one evening watching Victor play on the carpet in front of them. It was a lovely night and the sun was setting over a shimmering sea that poured delicate yellow and blue rays around the outline of the Isle of Capri in the distance. Mary was fascinated by the scene and hardly noticed when Victor began to play with her purse. It was a little game in which he often indulged, playfully teasing his mother with treasures he could find. In the purse. He first brought out the lipstick tube, then the little mirrored compact, handing each of the items to his father who joined in the game to please Victor. Guiseppe would take each item and move them from fist to fist, then challenge Victor to guess its location.

Mary was contentedly gazing out to sea and not watching the play when Victor withdrew the scrunched up piece of paper and gave it to Guiseppe to hide. Guiseppe idly began to flatten it out, simply to see if it contained anything of value, and fully intending to throw it away. He was reading it before Mary realized what was happening. When she saw the letter she was shocked to see what had happened.

'Juice's' face showed more sadness than anger, "Please Mary, what has happened? Who wrote this?"

Mary could not reply at first, she was stricken with remorse at the thought of her own unfaithfulness to her marriage. Finally she burst into tears and Guiseppe had to put his arms around her before she would stop weeping long enough to talk.

"This was a man I met during the war, in Harrowdale," she confessed. "He was stationed, no he was in a work camp for Italian prisoners of war at the hall. I ran into him in Rome one day."

'Juice was afraid to ask and really did not want to know, what secrets they might have had. His main concern was the fact that this stranger wanted to come to Sorrentoto see Mary, but he had even greater misgivings over the mention of State Security and of the party. "why does he want to come to Sorrento? What does he want with us here?"

Mary could not find it within herself to tell 'Juice' at this time. She would need time to set her life and her priorities aright before she could lay her whole life at his feet like this. "He probably won't come anyway. I hope he won't, Juice, I don't want to see him any more. He's high up in the Communists, I think."

Guiseppe was comforted somewhat to hear this from his wife. It seemed to lift the dark curtain of doubt, which he had experienced, and he longed to believe his wife's statement that she did not want to see this man again.

"then we'll burn the letter as Vittorio wanted you to do, and we'll forget about it once and for all, my dear." He went to the fireplace, struck a match, held it to the letter until it burst into flame and threw the burning paper into the fireplace.

He sat down beside her on the sofa once again, and took her into his arms, kissing her long and fervently, while she valiantly tried to respond. Victor crawled up to join in the hugging, and this more than anything else served to release the tension.

Guiseppe could not get this ghostly spectre, for that was what it amounted to, out of his mind. Who was this dangerous figure coming between him and his marriage. Was he a Communist, masquerading as a Secret Service man, or a Secret Service operative masquerading as a Communist? If he was a Communist out to create unrest in his factories, he might be able to put some protection money out to the Mafia and have him put away. But if he was a Secret Service man, in the employ of the Social

Democrats in government, he probably had just as many contacts and it would be dangerous to try to interfere with him. He made some discreet inquiries.

He longed to ask Mary about this man who presented such a dangerous threat to his marriage, but he did not want to remind her again. Instead he drove to Naples one day where he knew he would be able to make contact with his Mafia operative, the man who guaranteed him his labor peace in his factories. The connection in Naples did not know of any man of that name in the organization, but finally, he was identified by an operative in Rome as being the head of one of the most active Communist cells in the capital. This would make him doubly dangerous, not only was he a threat to his personal life, he was a man who could spread unrest in his work places, and in the whole area for that matter.

"We'll have our own security at your house then," said Tauro, his Mafia contact. "You want us to make it uncomfortable for him, don't you?"

"Just convince him not to stay here," said Guiseppe, "I wouldn't want to be responsible for anything drastic."

"We'll look after it for you," Tauro assured him, "and hey, when have we ever had to resort to drastic?"

Vittorio used the time during which he had to be in hiding from his Communist companions to make himself familiar with the Alamo Coast and with Sorrento in particular. Secret Service records showed that Sorrento was largely a Mafia free town, even though Naples, just thirty miles away, was a hotbed. The Communists had made no inroads whatsoever, as they had in the industrial area north of Rome. He could have used the government Mafia connections to give himself safe passage in Naples and Sorrento, but he preferred to travel with his other persona, that of a Communist organizer. The fact that he dared to invade this territory would further augment his image as a brave and loyal party worker.

He wore the open shirt and jeans favored by Communist party members and for this occasion, the party had provided him with an old Fiat to drive. It was a far cry from the Alfa Romeo and a challenge on these mountain roads where one had to maintain a decent speed.

He drove first to Naples. The first stop light he encountered turned suddenly red, causing him to brake hard, only to be loudly cursed by the driver behind, who had been intent on running the red light. It was a fitting introduction to the Naples scene.

Next a street urchin, armed with a dirty rag and a dirtier pail of water ran up and demanded to be allowed to wash his windscreen. He agreed, and while the boy cleaned he asked him where a nice cheap hotel could be arranged.

"Santa Lucia best," offered the boy, Hotel Rex." He pointed back in the direction from which he had come. Santa Lucia was a suburb on the outskirts of Naples.

"Turn here" said the young urchin, and he expertly stopped the oncoming traffic so that Vittorio could make a U turn. He was too embarrassed not to attempt this awkward maneuver, and he turned, oblivious to the shouts and curses of the drivers who had to wait.

When he had settled in his room, he phoned the Alano residence. To his delight Mary answered, "Guess where I am staying," he whispered to her, "in Santa Lucia, the real Santa Lucia, in the hotel Rex.

Luckily Guiseppe had gone to work that day, leaving her with Victor. She glanced outside to see that 'Juice's' car had left then said, "I've not told any one about us Vittorio, but your letter was in my purse when I got home and Victor found it, and before I knew it, he had given it to Guiseppe. I told Guiseppe that you were in the Communist party, and nothing more. Did I do right?"

"Yes my dear, it was the best thing to do. I'm sorry he had to find the letter, though. Tell me, does your husband have any thing to do with the Mafia, do you know?"

"He pays them to keep his factories clean, he says, and he does the same for my factory. He calls it money well spent."

"Can you get away long enough to come here to see me Mary?"

"Yes I might be able to. But I have heard some terrible things about that Santa Lucia place.

I would rather not go there."

"Then don't my dear, I have seen enough of Naples already, and this is one of the worst parts. I will have to come to Sorrento to see you."

"You must be very careful Vittorio. Guiseppe and his family are very powerful down here. I have the feeling that he has people watching me, ever since he found that letter in my purse."

"My darling, I long to see you. We have waited too long for this day, both of us."

There was a noise on the line, which made Vittorio wary. He had had much experience with spy operations over telephone lines. He hung up immediately, putting the receiver down solidly, then quietly and carefully picked it up to listen surreptitiously.

Mary was suddenly aware of the interruption from her end too, and she called, "Hello, hello, is anybody there?"

"Oh, I'm so sorry," said Anna Alano, "I just came in the door and I forgot to phone my friend today. I didn't mean to interrupt, dear."

Anna Alano was standing at the phone in the front hall while Mary had been using the extension in her bedroom upstairs.

"Oh, it's you Mama, I didn't hear you come in. It's quite all right. I was finished. Do you want to use the phone now?"

It was not quite all right and in fact Mary was 'quite' annoyed at her mother in law for sneaking into her house unannounced. She would speak to 'Juice about it as soon as he got home.

Vittorio put his receiver down softly, he had heard enough.

Mary would not dare to ask just how much her mother in law had actually heard. Anna had heard everything, she had contacted Tauro, of the Mafia and Tauro had decided to do his duty.

Within an hour three men visited the Rex Hotel in Santa Lucia and asked for Vittorio's room number. One of them cleverly picked the lock on the door of the room, and silently all three slipped inside. A man standing by the wash basin was shaving. When he saw the reflection of the three in the mirror he turned belligerently to defend himself but it was too late. A chloroform soaked rag was held over his face until he lost consciousness. He was laid over his bed and two wine bottles were emptied over him. The bed was soaked in kerosene, then as all three left by the door, a match was thrown onto the bedclothes. The door was closed and relocked with the key and the men ran down the stairway into the open. They watched until the flames exploded from the room on the fourth floor, smiled to each other indicating their pride in a well executed plan, and drove away.

Word of the success of the operation reached Guiseppe at his leather factory. He had not counted on so violent a reaction, a simple warning to stay away from his family might have been sufficient, but at least now he knew what the Mafia meant by protection. No one would dare to interfere with his family life.

He waited until the evening papers arrived with the news story of the fire in the Rex Hotel. Casually, he opened the paper at that page and left it folded on the sofa. When Mary came down from putting Victor to bed, she could not help but see the gruesome story. There was no list of casualties but there was fear that many of the guests of the hotel had been burnt to death. The fear and horror she felt was heightened when she realized that 'Juice was watching for her reaction.

"Is anything wrong, Mary?" 'Juice tried his utmost to speak calmly, but she could tell that he was making an effort to appear innocent.

"Not that I know of," she replied, "I see there has been a fire in the Rex Hotel again. I wonder who was burnt alive this time."

"I have no idea my dear. It was a very run down place anyway. Probably just a few tramps or Communists."

Mary had heard enough. The word Communist had convinced her that Guiseppe knew all about her phone conversation that morning with Vittorio. She began to put together the noise on the phone line and then the protestations of innocence as Anna her mother in law had come into her house. But how could they have reacted so quickly? And now the paper opened at precisely the headline he knew she would have dreaded. Guiseppe actually gloating inwardly, she suspected, and the thought of it repulsed her.

"I'm going to my room," she announced, "I'm very tired and I don't feel well tonight."

"I'm very sorry my dear" said 'Juice'. "I was hoping we could have a talk tonight."

Mary did not even reply. She went upstairs to her room hoping that Guiseppe would stay downstairs until she had at least gone to sleep.

Chapter Ten

▼

Reconciled

When Vittorio put his phone back in its receptacle he sat quietly for a few seconds. Instintively, he knew someone had been listening to his conversation with Mary. If this husband of hers really had connections with the Mafia, they would be sure to react promptly, especially like this on a matter of family honour. Slowly, he walked downstairs to the hotel office. He cheerily said hello to the room clerk, saying, "nice day today, isn't it?" as he began to turn the pages of the guest register. Seeing his own name and the fact that he was registered in Room 4, he corrected the entry, mumbling a little rueful comment about the fact that no one seemed to know how to spell 'Babando' correctly. To a casual observer, it would seem that he had corrected the spelling of his own name, whereas in reality he had simply added a one in front of his room number, changing the register to read that he was in Room 14. He left the building altogether and crossed the street to stand and watch. He had only a few minutes to wait.

Three men entered the lobby, moving directly towards the registration counter. One of the men reached across for the guest register, studied it for a short time, then all three went up the stairs. Suddenly Vittorio saw smoke emanating from the room above his. The men came running out to the street, as the window shattered and bright red flames burst forth. The three raced to their van and sped away.

The room clerk rushed out from the building and into the street, his hands raised in a signal for help. A policeman ran to his aid and then blew his whistle to stop the traffic while the room clerk ran to a telephone to call for the Fire Department.

For the next hour and a half, it was a scene of frantic activity as firemen rushed to set out their hoses and ambulances hove into view to pick up the dead and the wounded. Within two hours, the building had collapsed in on itself and was a smoking pile of black ash.

There must have been someone in that room, Vittorio speculated, he could not get over the feeling that he had condemned someone to death. He shuddered to think that this action was probably meant for himself. "My God what a family has she gotten into," thought he, "she deserves to be free of these people, once and for all."

He had seen cold blooded killing by the Mafia more than once before in his work at State Security, but it had always been an impersonal thing to him since it was directed against the Communists most of the time in the North. He had spent years infiltrating the Communist party in the belief that they were the most dangerous menace to the country, only to find that the threat to the country's stability was far more serious from the Mafia itself.

He saw the clerk coming towards him, somewhat dazed and dirty with smoke blackened hands and face, carrying a large ledger, the hotel register, which he had managed to save from the wreckage. Vittorio turned his back so that the clerk walked past without recognizing him, straight towards a group of policemen. Vittorio edged closer so that he might eavesdrop on the conversation.

"Here is the register of guests," said the clerk.

"How many died, can you give me their names?" The constable asked. "I don't know for certain yet, constable," said the clerk, but it looks as if the fire started in Room 14, that would be the room occupied by a man named Vittorio Babando, according to this room register. He did not get out."

"What happened, was he smoking, do you think?"

"I'm not sure, he had three visitors, just before the fire broke out of his room."

"Three visitors!" said one of the police. "Can you give us a description?"

"They came in a black van, it was parked across the street. They left in a hurry, I noticed, in the same van.

The policeman's eyes widened, then he turned to his companions, "so that's it, a Mafia job. What can we do, nothing.

Someone's got in their way. Let them settle it then."

Vittorio shrank back into the burgeoning group of spectators, losing himself in the crowd. Technically then, he did not exist any more. Vittorio Babando had lost his life in a hotel fire. He was free, free to live his own life at last. Not once since the war had he been able to say this of himself. He had been a prisoner of the system, not daring to reveal himself, living the double life of a government informant and masquerading at the same time as a loyal supporter of the communists and an advocate of the revolution of the masses.

Now he could live his own life, free of all the forces pulling Italy apart, but where? Where would he go? He would leave Italy of course, join the move to the New World, maybe, even go to America,or anywhere, as long as he was free of both the Mafia and the Communists.

Where, in all of Italy could he lose himself? Not in Rome certainly, he knew too many people and too many knew him. Naples and Sorrento were out of the question. In Venice he could be trapped on a canal one day with no escape route. Wait a minute! how about Florence? It would be closer to home in Parma and it's big enough to become lost in its piazzas. On top of all that, there was the home office of the San Raphael Department Store, and it's manager, Mr. Jorge Boscolini. Boscolini had been his superior officer during the war, and would still be a good friend. They had joined up, fought and been taken prisoner together. His best chance of anonymity was definitely in Florence. He retrieved the little Fiat from it's parking stall and headed north on the road to Roma. According to Mary, J. Boscolini still held him in high regard.

But he wanted Mary to be free too, most of all he wanted Mary to come with him, wherever he went. Somehow he would have to let her know that he cared, that he was free to care for her for the rest of her life. It was truly astounding the way his love for her was re-awakened. When he left England he had left because it was his sworn duty to his country, and all else had to stand aside. Those weeks when he knew her in England had been precious to him but he had thought of it as a mere pleasant interlude, and one that she would have forgotten too.

He had never known the reality of a happy family life. In all these years of living, his only pleasure had been that of the thrill of the risks he had been forced to run in his every day existence.

He thought grimly that the Mafia had almost robbed him of this. He had come that close to being one of their victims. Many times up north, when the Social Democrats had trouble with unions he had directed the Mafia to the headquarters of the Communist party, to the union heads. He had thought of this as his patriotic duty before, but now the doubts which he had to suppress as a member of the Secret Service again began to assail him. He had the chance to break the cycle once and for all, but this time he must include Mary and his son in his plans.

Many times in the next few days the telephone rang in her house but when she answered she could hear nothing except heavy breathing in the receiver. She decided not to answer it at all. Once, it rang when her mother in law, Anna Alano was in the house. Mrs. Alano was greeted by the same stony silence, which caused her to think that perhaps the call had been for Mary alone.

She asked Mary if someone had been calling her privately, someone who was not liked by Giuseppe, perhaps. Mary became quite annoyed at what amounted to an accusation of unfaithfulness from her mother in law, and said so, in no uncertain terms. The very next day, when she was alone in the house, the phone rang again. She picked up the receiver and fairly shouted into the receiver, "Hello there." and listened.

At first no sound came. She held the receiver and out of the silence came an instantly recognizable tune being whistled. It was the last few bars of 'Santa Lucia'. She gripped the receiver tightly when she heard the unmistakeable tenor voice singing the last fading words of the melody, "Santa Lucia." Then suddenly, the line went dead.

She glanced around to make sure Anna Alano was not within hearing distance and whispered excitedly, "Vittorio!, Vittorio," but there was no answer.

With a tremendous sigh of relief, Mary put down the phone. "He's not dead, he's alive!" she thought. "Oh, thank god, thank god!".

Even Giuseppe noticed the change in his wife's attitude and was moved to remark on her cheerful disposition. He and his mother happily told each other that Mary had become a good Italian housewife at last. A new family was sure to follow, thought Anna. They found it curious that Mary had suddenly taken to humming the Santa Lucia chorus, but since it seemed to make her feel better it became a favorite refrain throughout the house.

When she had heard nothing more for the next month, Mary began to have some doubts. She began to wonder if this had been an imagined thing, this phone call. Did she really receive one?

Not a soul knew, Mary remembered, except her girl friend Gloria, that this was the secret theme song for Vittorio and her, and Gloria was back in England. She hadn't even spoken to Gloria for years so in all the wide world the only person who could have sung that song to her at that moment was Vittorio. He had not been killed in the hotel fire, after all, he must be safe and well, but where?

She longed to go to Naples, to Rome even, to find him, but now she was being closely watched by the Alano family. In fact, she was a virtual prisoner in her own household. She could not even phone to the factory without hearing sounds of breathing through the connections. Every phone call was being monitored.

To all of this Victor was kept completely unaware. His step father, Guiseppe was even more attentive these days, constantly bringing him things to play with from town, and taking him for exciting rides on his scooter practically every evening. It was becoming increasingly difficult for her to suggest another trip to England even, because Victor seemed to want his 'father' to be with him constantly.

Mary was quite used to getting phone calls from both her suppliers and her customers during her days at the factory. One day, she answered a call from Florence and was pleasantly surprised to find that it was Mr. Boscolini, the president of the San Raphael Department Store. He was most anxious that she see his new women's department, which was now featuring the For Mother's line. "I have just been appointed President, Mrs. Alano and we would like to hold a sale of clothing especially for new mothers and mothers-to-be. I believe your line would fit into our sale plans perfectly. Possibly you could come to Florence yourself and show us the best of your new creations."

Mary had been waiting for some excuse to go to Rome by herself possibly, or better still, a reason to take Victor to England. She dearly wanted to take him away from the Alanos family, but Florence of all places was not on her list of priorities.

"I might find it rather difficult to get away at this time of year," she objected. Boscolini was quiet for a moment, then he began to speak slowly and carefully, so that Mary could almost feel the presence of another person in his office. "There is a wonderful place here to buy the most exquisite tartufo, Mrs. Alano. Does your son like tartufos?"

Of course every child in Italy loved a tartufo, of that there was absolutely no doubt, but wait, what had made him think of Victor? And who had told him about Victor's love for tartufo? There was only one way, it had to be.

She could hardly disguise the excitement when she said, "he loves them Mr. Boscolini, do you think he would like the ones in Florence?"

"I am absolutely certain of it, Mrs Alano, and I am sure we would enjoy having him."

She did not dare to ask what he meant by the term "we", but she was heartened when next he told her, "one of my boys would be very happy to look after him for you, while you and I work on the line, Mrs. Alano. As a matter of fact he asked me to make sure that you brought your son with you."

He was silent for a moment, then said to Mary, "can you hear what I am hearing?"

Faintly, in the distance she could hear the words sung once more, the last two words of the familiar chorus, "Santa Lucia!"

"Yes," said Mary, "of course I'll come. I'll be only to happy to help you. I think I can give you some ideas which we used in England in our stores."

Excitedly, she told Guiseppe of her plans to go to Florence. He thought it might be a good opportunity to go along with her and they could plan a joint promotion with his leather goods. She thought of saying that she could not jeopardize her dress sale for the sake of a few leather belts but that would be altogether too rude and callous. Instead, she said, "I want to see if he likes our new line of dresses for young ladies not just the expandable waist kind, Juice, and I'd like to see if we could get him started looking at our children's outfits. too. I think I would rather handle this myself this time. I'm sorry Juice, but you always find it so boring and slow, don't you?".

Mary's enthusiasm for her trip to Florence mounted daily. She excitedly told Guiseppe how important this would be for the business, how the season's future depended on this important showing. He agreed but for the life of him could not see why Victor had to be taken. "Good Heavens," said he, "Victor should be able to get along without you and you without him by now. He will be quite safe here with me."

Her plans to take Victor with her on her promotional trip encountered much stronger objections, from his mother, Anna Alano.

Anna Alano was even more suspicious than her son. When she heard that Mary wanted to take Victor along, it seemed to her that her daughter-in-law wanted to separate herself from her rightful family, that she was afraid that Victor was becoming more Italian than English. She was almost certain that there was some ulterior motive, even though all the evidence pointed to this man whom she knew had been killed in the hotel fire.

Mrs. Alano had a more sinister reason for objecting. "There's something to this trip I don't like. I wonder if she has met another of her boy friends."

Giuseppe scolded her for thinking such things, "she would be naturally upset if this man was such a good friend. I wish Tauro had not been so cruel myself. He did not deserve to be murdered, you know."

Mary let Victor take some of his prized toys along on their trip, for there was extra space in the sample suitcases which she took along for Mr. Boscolini's displays. She worked for three evenings in selecting the stock which she would take with her. Many of the dresses which she carried were her own size so that she had a sizeable wardrobe for herself. She had packed most of the suitcases herself at her office at the factory and had them shipped directly to the San Raphael department store.

Giuseppe came to the station to see them off. "Are you sure that you want to make this trip alone, Mary? Please promise me that you will call me if you need any kind of help. Remember I have many good friends, in the North too."

"I'll remember, Juice," Mary replied, "and I promise to call if I need any help." The mental picture of the Mafia protection ring which was at this moment all around her, clouded her thoughts as she replied. It was on the day after Mary and Victor left that Anna Alano noticed a news item in the daily paper from Naples which read, HOTEL ROOM REGISTER ERROR LEADS TO IDENTIFICATION OF FIRE VICTIM.

The story told of the Rex Hotel room clerk's error which at first indicated that the person losing his life in Room 14 had been one Vittorio Babando, but that the dental records of the body had shown it to be that of one Simone Paulo, an itinerant laborer. The clerk had claimed that either he had registered Mr. Babando in No.14 in error, or someone had changed the register on purpose.

Anna Alano took the newspaper to her son's house. "See Giuseppe, maybe he is not dead after all. Maybe you should send Tauro to Florence to see what is going on!"

Chapter Eleven

▼

Meeting

Giuseppe decided to phone Tauro, his Mafia contact. He felt that some explanation should be forthcoming for the burning of a hotel and the loss of innocent lives. He knew that he should accord Tauro the respect he was due as a Mafia boss.,Men of his kind did not take kindly to slurs against their ability or reputation. This time however, Giuseppe was genuinely annoyed and his tone showed it.

"Tauro," said Giuseppe, "what have you dirty wretches been up to? You've killed some poor brick layer now, and for no good reason. Why were you so sloppy? I thought you told me you would be more careful."

"You wanted him out of your way, didn't you? You told us he was only a Commie scab. We get rid of all the Commies in Naples. We always do!"

"But you missed him, missed him completely. Instead you manage to get some poor guy called Simone Paulo, who never even had a chance.
What are you going to say to his family?"

"He happened to get in the way, that's all. How was I to know some stupid bastard would make a mess of the room register? If you want to blame someone, blame the room clerk in the Rex. What the hell are you so excited about anyway, we must have scared the living daylights out of this Vittorio, or you'd have seen him around by now. He's probably left town so fast he forgot his clothes! Ha ha, they're burnt anyway."

"Very funny, Tauro," said Giuseppe, "what if that poor fellow Paulo had a wife and kids?"

"What's more important?" Tauro replied, "some woman you don't even know like that guy's wife or your own wife and family?"

"All right, all right, talking about my own wife, she's left on a trip to Florence, a business trip, but she has taken her son with her. I want you to make sure she's safe."

"I know what you mean, Giuseppe, you want to make sure this guy Vittorio Babando doesn't turn up in Florence, don't you?"

"Well, yes, I do, but why do you have to be so untidy? God, if another hotel burns down, you might kill a whole bunch this time."

"We've got a job to do, we do it. What do you want us to do?" "Just let me know that my wife and her son are safe, that's all.

And let me know if she meets anyone else in Florence. My mother is suspicious as hell, she thinks that Mary is going to meet someone. And when I think of it all, she might be right."

"This time, I'll go myself," said Tauro, "all the way to Florence, even though it's not my territory. I know someone there I can make contact with. Now, what do we do if we find this Vittorio there, and he's shacked up with Mary."

"Goddammit, he won't be, Mary would never ah," Giuseppe hesitated a moment, gathering his thoughts. "Phone me if you find him there, phone me right away, I want to deal with it myself."

Mr. Boscolini was waiting on the station platform for Mary and Victor when she arrived at the Florence Stazione. He rushed over to greet her and she found herself taken into a happy group of people. on the station platform. She was introduced to first Boscolini's wife and then to his young teen-aged family. She glanced anxiously around the group of people, hoping that she would see someone else she knew. Boscolini saw that she was concerned, and moved to comfort her.

"Please allow me to take your suitcases, Mrs. Alano," said J. Boscolini,

"I'll be most happy to take you and your son to your hotel, if you'll accept our assistance."

"Why that's most gracious of you, Mr. Boscolini," Mary replied, "I hope you don't mind if I have our displays shipped to directly to your store."

"That will be excellent, Madame Alano, we'll go straight to my car then."

Mary expected that Boscolini would have a chauffeur but he did not. Instead, he took the driver's seat himself, his wife beside him, and the chauffeur instead drove a limousine which contained his four children, three young boys and a thirteen year old daughter. The four children were if anything, pleased that they had the chauffeur to themselves. There was much laughing and playful bantering amongst them, and Mary could see that they were giving the poor chauffeur a difficult time. Boscolini shouted a caution to his children and admonished the chauffeur to report any sign of misbehaviour. The chauffeur drove away and Mary could well imagine that the children would be enjoying themselves to the full before the limousine had travelled the length of the block.

Mary seated herself in the back of the Boscolini family car, a comfortable Lancia sedan, with Victor sitting beside her. Just as they were about to leave the station, a man came running out of the waiting room, and quickly got into the back of the Lancia without a word of explanation. He gently lifted Victor onto his knee and sat with him next to Mary as Boscolini sped away from the station. Mary uttered a startled little word of alarm and then, as she looked at the intruder and recognised him, she whispered, "Vittorio, you really are safe!"

"Yes my dear, but only for the moment," said Vittorio, "I drove here only yesterday, sold the little Communist car, the Fiat and now I'm staying with the Boscolinis. I don't want to be seen in public because that family of yours in Sorrento have many connections in the Mafia, and I cannot take too many chances."

"Perhaps, Mrs. Alano, you would like to come to my house, so that you could make some plans together. We could always take you to your hotel later in the evening, and then you would be safe from the prying eyes."

"What prying eyes?" asked Mary.

"The prying eyes of the Mafia, Mrs Alano, they are every—where and anywhere, it seems. By the way where are you staying in Florence, may I ask?"

"My husband has booked a suite at the Relais Certosa for me," said Mary, "he tells me that it is a nice quiet place which looks out onto a park."

"Aha, a wise choice indeed, it is secluded as well and easy to drive to and for the little boy, there is a swimming pool," said J.Boscolini. "You will love it there, I am sure."

"And you, Vittorio," asked Mary, "have you a place to stay?" "He will be staying with us, Mrs. Alano, Vittorio and I have talked of many things over the last few days. We both remember the pleasant little English town of Harrowdale."

Mrs. Boscolini had taken no part in the conversation until that time, but she still knew of the unique relationship. She smiled an assurance to Mary, saying, "Yes Mary, they have spent many hours talking to each other, and now I believe that you and Vittorio have much to talk of also."

Vittorio reached over and squeezed Mary's hand which caused her to blush for the first time in many years. Her blush was immediately perceived by Mrs. Boscolini and she smiled appreciatively.

"For the first time in my whole life, I think, I can say that I am completely without care", said Vittorio. "Since the hotel fire in which I was supposedly burned to death, I find myself without a single concern and I must say it is a most relaxing feeling.

It must be like this when a person retires, I suppose."

"It will be most gratifying to the people in your department in Rome when they find that you are alive after all," said Boscolini. "How long have you worked for them in the security service? I am told on the highest authority that your services have been invaluable. You must be very proud of your work there."

"I would rather have, much rather have been in your position, Jorge, and not have to be in a constant struggle against all the forces which would try to destroy the country like the Fascisti and the Communists. Personally, I am sick to death of it all, and now at last, I have a chance to be free of it. I'm officially dead, you see, I hope I never see the Security Department again I'm going to take this chance and disappear forever!"

"You would be best to leave Italy altogether then," said Boscolini, because the Communist or the Mafia will find you out in this country, you can depend on that."

"If only Mary and I can have a few days by ourselves. How about that, Mary Holdwell?" he said suddenly, turning to Mary, and addressing her by her maiden name, the name by which he had known her in England. "There is so much to see in Florence, and I would be happy to take you to see some of our famous sights, the works of Leonardo da Vinci and Michelangelo, and the ancient home of the Medici."

"Oh Vittorio, there is so much to think of. And this is after all, a working holiday for me, you know. Mr. Boscolini expects me to show my lines to his people."

"Mary, you need have no worry there at all. I can have my managers display your lines quite well and you may be assured of a sizeable order from San Raphael this time," said J. Boscolini.

The car was nearing Boscolini's villa. It was on a rise of land which afforded an excellent view of the Arno River and the Ponte Vecchio. It was an ancient building, surrounded by classic columns and the car drew up before the imposing doorway.

"This is our town house, where we can have a bit of lunch before we take you to your hotel, Mrs. Alano," said Mrs. Boscolini, "Your hotel is not far away, just a ten minute drive on the Via Romana, and your son will enjoy it there too. He will have lots of fun in the swimming pool, I'm sure.

When they were settled in the parlour with their tea, and Mrs. Boscolini had made a dish of ice cream for Victor, Vittorio asked Mary to come sit by him so they could talk and make some plans. Mary took a toy from her purse for Victor to play with and he sat contentedly on the floor playing.

Vittorio began to unburden himself to Mary, "I can leave the Secret Service now and I will," said he, "they have put me down as deceased, and I am free at last, but I might have to leave Italy."

"Can't you just wash your hands of the whole mess, Vittorio and do something else."

"I know too much, Mary, too much of their inner circle and the joke of the whole thing is that the Mafia group down there in Sorrento think I am just another Communist. They had no idea I was working undercover."

"But there is something else, Vittorio. The phone call which my mother-in-law heard in Sorrento convinced her that you are a threat to my marriage to Giuseppe Alano, and she and Giuseppe alerted the Mafia about it."

"That could be worse than ever then, for now the Mafia are protecting a family, and that is a matter of honor."

"Perhaps it is just as well that you are officially dead, Vittorio." "Just the same, you can be sure that you have been followed here, and since your husband knows where you will be staying, it is better that we meet here. What is to become of us, Mary?"

"Vittorio, you will never know how much I wanted this to happen, how long I have waited for you, and now I feel positively wicked for feeling the way I do."

"Then it's settled, Mary, we're together, forever. Nothing will part us, ever."

"Vittorio, that's exactly what you promised in Harrowdale."

"I know Mary, but this time, I am free and nothing will come between us."

"But can we live here in Italy?"

"I'm afraid not, my dear, the Mafia would hardly allow it.

Maybe some day, when the Mafia is no more, and the Communist have broken up, we can move back. It is too bad, Italy is so beautiful!"

"Oh yes Vittorio, it is, I love it here, especially the Amalfi Coast, and Sorrento is beautiful. Maybe some day, we can come back to live on Capri?"

He took her into his arms and they became locked in a long, passionate kiss. Victor looked up wonderingly, "doing mother?" he asked. They were oblivious to his question. Even Mrs.Boscolini's entrance into the room failed to break the embrace, and she tip toed out again.

Mary whispered finally, "I must get to my hotel to check in, Vittorio."

"I'll drive you there, if I can borrow Jorge's car," said Vittorio.

"Oh no you mustn't be seen around my hotel, Vittorio."

"I'll borrow the chauffeur's cap, and we'll take the limousine. That way they'll not recognise me."

Mary thanked the Boscolinis for all their help and Vittorio arranged with the chauffeur to borrow his car for half an hour.

Vittorio, in his role as chauffeur, carried Mary's luggage to her room. He quietly closed the door and they stood in the room and embraced once more, until they heard Victor once again ask, "doing Mother?"

"Oh look Vittorio, they have left a copy of today's paper on the desk for me." There's a story on the fire at the Rex Hotel in Naples. The headline read

'POSITIVE IDENTIFICATION OF VICTIM THROUGH DENTAL RECORDS' and the story told how the victim, who had first been identified as Vittorio Babando because of the room records salvaged from the flames, had now been proved to have been those of Simone Paulo through examination of dental records. No trace of Vittorio Babando has been found since.

They read the article in silence, then Vittorio, his face ashen, looked into Mary's eyes, "it seems there's no rest for the wicked, my dear."

"The people in Security will be on the lookout for you, Vittorio, they know you're alive so you had better tell them where you are."

"Yes Mary, and the Communists will know also. My cover is blown with them so they will be looking for me, and they would be just as happy if I *was b*urnt to death."

Vitorrio thought a minute as he read the date on the masthead of the paper, then said, "that is yesterday's paper. The news must have been known in Naples two days ago and they would have had time to send someone up here to watch for me."

"Then you'd best go back to Boscolini's dear, before they discover it's you and not just a chauffeur."

"I hate to think I will be leaving you alone here, Mary."

"I'm not alone Vittorio, I have Victor with me and my husband knows I'm staying here, so it will be perfectly safe for me here."

"Tell me Mary, does your husband love you as much as I do. If he does he will be very angry, most exceedingly angry with me, and there is nothing I can do about it."

"I know Vittorio, I know, but I do think that Juice and I had a more or less of a marriage of convenience. It was convenient for him because my factories and his complement each other. He was about to be forced by his family to marry someone within his church, and his marriage to me was an escape really. His mother manages his every move. She spies on me whenever she can and it was often quite depressing to live that closely to her. I must say though, that she was good to Victor and he worships her and Victor looks upon Giuseppe as his father too."

Vittorio looked down at Victor, as he playfully began to tear the newspaper from top to bottom. "Look at those chubby little hands, Mary, he's going to have big ham hands like mine when he grows up. I'll do my best to make him love me as his father, I promise."

"I'm sure you will Vittorio, and when he is old enough to see the likeness between you it will become easy for both of you. Just look at those ears, Vittorio."

"Yes, Mary it is astonishing, said Vittorio, fingering his own ear, "but I had better go back to Boscolini's and not stay in this room a minute longer. It is far too long for a chauffeur to be here as it is," he said with a smile.

"Arrivaderci, Victor," he called. Victor was absorbed in his paper games and Mary took him by the hand to say goodbye to Vittorio. Vittorio lifted him high in the air and tickled him in the tummy in the process. He clapped his hands and when he was finally put down again he put his hands in the air, entreating Vittorio to "do it again, do it again!"

"You had better be off, Vittorio," said Mary, holding Victor in check.

Going through the lobby by himself, Vittorio looked carefully around the room trying to spot anyone who did not seem to fit the touristy pattern. He did see two men sitting on a settee who appeared to be hiding behind a newspaper rather than reading. One of them looked up, spotted his chauffeur cap, and looked down at his paper once more. They looked suspiciously like the men who had come into the Rex Hotel in Naples. He walked quickly to the door, not daring to look back until he went out. They were talking animatedly between themselves as he unlocked the door of the limousine and they were standing at the window watching him as he left.

Vittorio phoned back to the Relais Certosa Hotel to tell Mary that he had seen the two men from Naples in the lobby of the Hotel. "They are keeping guard over you, I expect, and they watched me drive away in the limousine so they know Boscolini's cars too, it seems."

"Are these the men from Naples, do you think?" Mary had to marvel at the speed with which the mafia men had traced her.

"Your husband would have told them where you are staying," said Vittorio.

"Maybe you could tell them that you are not a Communist, after all, and that you have some connections of your own."

"I would never convince them of that, these guys need their own kind to do the convincing. They are on a mission to protect one of their own, Giuseppe Alano, they think that his marriage is in danger, and that I am the culprit, the guilty party in this thing. They can be dangerous, I think I'll contact Security and have them get in touch with some of the men up north here. The Naples branch knows that they can't operate in Florence."

The next morning Mary's phone in her room rang early waking her. It was Juice inquiring for her safety, and asking once again if he could help with the showings. Mary assured him that everything was running smoothly, and that his help was not needed. "Mary, I have just finished making a new leather coating line. It is a new departure for us and I have used some of your pattern people to help me put it together. I would like to show it to the San Raphael people to get their reaction. You know, before we go into production. Now since you are already there, and talking to the buyers, I am going to come to Florence to show the line. It will go with your lines perfectly, Mary."

It was all a ruse and an excuse to come to Florence, Mary knew, but she tried valiantly not to let her anger show. Juice had been working on this outerwear project for a year and the garments were going to prove too costly to make with the limited supplies he had available. "I don't think you should be promoting that now with winter coming," she said. "It would be better to introduce it in Spring for Christmas sales."

Giuseppe was quite familiar with the buying patterns of the large department stores, who always made their buying decisions six months in advance, but he was determined to be in Florence. "Mary, I'm coming to Florence. I know that you have met this man whom you knew in England there and I am quite disappointed in you. I must see you at once."

It was all out in the open now. "Juice, you can tell your spies to stay away from me. I warn you, Juice, I have powerful friends here who will not stand for this kind of treatment. Juice? Juice? Are you there Juice? Do you hear me?"

The phone connection had gone dead, and she put the receiver down with a crash herself.

Back at the Boscolini residence, Vittorio phoned to his official State Security office in Rome. His secretary was not a little surprised to hear his voice, and greatly pleased that he was still alive and well. "It's wonderful to know that you're safe, Major," said Andrea, his secretary, "you'll have some explaining to do for the Communists, that's for sure."

"Where's the chief, Andrea?"

"In his office, Major, now are you listening to me? You had a close call, and the chief doesn't think."

"Give me the chief, Andrea, please."

The next voice to be heard was the chief 's, "who wants me?"

"It's Vittorio, chief."

"Back from the dead? Where are you now?"

"I'm in Florence, chief, and I need some help."

"Always ready to oblige, Vito, old boy, what's the problem?"

Vittorio spoke of the close call he had had in Sorrento and the persistence of the particular Mafia squad in tailing him to Florence. What are they doing up here, that's not their territory," replied the chief,

"It's not political at all, this time, Chief. In fact if the truth were told it is an affair of the heart."

"Of the heart? Not your heart, surely, Babando."

"I'm afraid so, chief. It is a dear friend from my days as a prisoner in England. She was beautiful then and she's even more beautiful now. And she has my son with her."

"So what's the problem?"

"She is married to a chap from Sorrento, who seems to be close to the Mafia in Naples."

He explained the reason for his close call in Naples and the ruthless methods taken to ensure that he was killed. "They are going to try some more of their tricks in Florence if we don't find a way to stop them."

"We can't have Mafia from Naples operating up north here. They're the worst kind, too bloodthirsty. Tell you what Vittorio, I'll get our man Arturo on it right away. He knows how to deal with the southern branch.

"Tell me Vito, when are you coming back to the office? We'll have to use you in a different job from now on, since your Communist cover is blown. The Commies will be out to get you. The only safe thing for you to do is join the Mafia yourself, the Commies will never dare to touch you then."

"Chief, I could never do that."

"You're a numbered person Vito. You know too much about the Communist and they don't trust you. And you know the inner secrets of the Mafia and they can't let you run around loose with all that. How about going into politics? May be you could be Prime Minister one day, if you handle your cards right."

"Thanks for the vote of confidence, chief, see you in a few days then. You'll have Arturo come to Florence, will you?"

"Sure thing, Vito."

CHAPTER TWELVE

▼

RESCUE

Mary sat at the phone for some minutes, half expecting Guiseppe to call back, because it would mean that he had taken her seriously, and was not coming to Florence. He did not call.

When the phone did ring the next morning, it was Vittorio, saying he would be bringing the Boscolini limousine over to pick them up for lunch. She told him of her call from Guiseppe, that Guiseppe knew all about her every move in Florence. "I'm afraid he might try to interfere with us some way."

Vittorio assured her that he had looked after these things. He had been in touch with his own office in Rome., he told her, and State Security would be taking over as of today. A man named Arturo would be looking after things in Florence. "He will take care of this Tauro whoever he is, and see that he goes back to Naples," said Vittorio.

"Is this Arturo from State Security or is he Mafia too?" She shouldn't have asked she knew, but she was curious.

"We have the Mafia here in the North too but they are better behaved than the Naples bunch.". They handle all of our problems with the Communists.

Mary dared not think of the consequences of two Mafia groups from different parts of the country suddenly meeting with diametrically opposed objectives.

Half an hour later, Vittorio arrived at the lobby entrance. He made his way into the hotel to meet Mary. Suddenly he heard a voice saying his name,"Vittorio Babando". He looked around quickly but could see noone he knew. The man who had spoken had seen Vittorio's turn of the head at hearing his name thus unknowingly verifying his identity. He had walked behind a large pillar, then unhurriedly left through the door, attracting no one's attention.

Once outside, the man waved a finger salute to his companion in a van parked close to the entrance.The passenger door opened from the inside and the man came out through the lobby door and entered the van. The man who had been sitting in the Driver's seat had got out and approached the limousine from behind, quickly bent down beneath the rear bumper, then just as quickly moved back to the van.

Just at that moment, Mary emerged from the lift with Victor holding tightly to her hand. She immediately saw the worried look on Vittorio's face, "What's wrong Vittorio, you look as if you had seen a ghost!"

"Someone here knows me," said Vittorio, whoever it was just called me by name, now I would like to see who it is."

They both looked around the room but the stranger would not show himself. A bell boy appeared to be calling several messages and one of the names he asked for was 'Maria Alano'. Mary identified herself and he stopped walking long enough to say "a message on the desk for you Madam", and to accept Mary's 50 Lira tip as he walked briskly away.

"I'll take Victor to the car while you get your message," said Vittorio, gathering the boy up in his arms and walking out to the limousine.

Mary hurried over to the desk for her message. The clerk looked in her box and withdrew a handwritten note. To her surprise it was a note from 'Juice'. It said simply,"I can't let you do this to me Mary. I love you and you are my wife. G"

She read and re-reads the note, wondering if he was there right at this moment, watching her read. A man came and stood beside her and when she at last raised her eyes to look at him it was Guiseppe!. His eyes were boring into her and his face was stern. "That note is from your husband, you know" he said, "and I am standing right beside you, trying to make you see some sense. Who is that man? Was that Vittorio Babando, the Communist? He is not for you, Mary."

Equally angry and startled though she felt at seeing 'Juice" she would like to have set him straight, to tell him that Vittorio was no Communist that he wielded much influence because really he was really a security officer in the government but this was hardly the time or for that matter the place for such talk.

She simply said, "I'm sorry 'Juice' but he has come back into my life, and there is nothing any one can do about it. I will tell you this Guiseppe, he is the real father of my child. He is Victor's father, and I must go to him."

"Please don't go to him now Mary, stay here and talk to me. We can work things out, I will make Victor my son and look after him better than a father such as your Vittorio ever would be able to.

"You're wrong 'Juice', Vittorio is very capable. He is a fine man and we intend to live together."

"My mother and my family will not stand for it. You cannot go back to Sorrento. My friends would not let him live there for a minute."

"Then I will not go back, Guiseppe." Suddenly Mary saw clearly into the future, and her future included Vittorio. "You can have the factory, and Vittorio and I will go to England to live. Now I must leave. Vittorio is waiting for me in the car outside."

"What have you done with Victor, Mary," asked Guiseppe, is he alone in your room This last question seemed to be asked rather fearfully and Mary's senses were alerted to some unseen danger. She quickly answered, "he is in the car with Vittorio, of course, Why?"

"In the car? With Vittorio? Do you mean that black limousine?" Mary had only time to nod 'yes' in response when Guiseppe ran for the door. He knocked down a lamp in his haste and sent a man flying sideways in his headlong struggle to get outside.

The door swung with such velocity that the glass shattered and the noise brought everyone to the front of the hotel.

In the street, the black limousine was parked directly at the front door. Victorrio was sitting in the driver's seat with Victor sitting in his lap. Guiseppe ran towards the limo. Signalling wildly to Vittorio to shut down the motor. Victorrio turned the key but he knew that it would be too late, that the bomb would be triggered. Guiseppe dove into the right hand seat and grasped Victor's arms, pulling him across the seat and out of the car. Vittorio dove from the left side of the car, rolled onto the pavement and underneath another car Guiseppe pushed Victor down and put himself into a fetal position to protect him.

The explosion shattered all of the windows facing the street. Flying glass formed shard like daggers which slashed curtains, drove daggers of glass into the lobby, piercing the upholstery and worst of all, driving into human flesh. There was a sudden silence, then screams of the injured could be heard, screams of agony, and groans of pain, as the people on the street called for help.

Mary's face stung from what seemed a thousand pin pricks as she desperately tried to make her way through the melee to the street. She was appalled at the scene outside, and she too began to scream when she realized that the limousine had been destroyed.

"Vittorio, Victor, where are you? What has happened!" She ran to the wrecked limousine and looked inside. It was resting on its roof. The wheels still spinning and a flame spurted from the gas tank.

Undeterred, she bent to look inside but she was pulled from the wreckage by someone who cautioned, "it's going to blow, the gas tank, better stay away."

"I can't help it," she shouted, "my son is in there, my son!"

"Sorry lady, there's nobody alive in there anymore," he replied as he gently moved her back. There's nothing anyone can do now."

A siren sounded the arrival of a police cruiser. The two constables in the cruiser surveyed the scene and immediately called for the fire department and for an ambulance. The square in front of the hotel was cordoned off to keep the curious away.

Mary sank to the curb and began to cry uncontrollably. She was oblivous to the screams and groans of the wounded and neither officers nor ambulance attendants had time to help her. She saw the terrible injuries which the explosion had inflicted but they meant nothing to her. She could not even sympathize with them. She watched the activity with a detached air as if she were a spectator to some terrible movie sequence. There was a groan which seemed to emanate from beneath a badly damaged car which had originally stood next to the limousine. A policeman looked beneath and called for assistance, "there's somebody trapped in here, help me lift the car."

Many hands volunteered and the car was turned over to reveal a man trapped under the drive shaft. He emerged blackened with oil but otherwise unscathed. He turned towards Mary and his face lit up in a white toothed smile as he knelt down beside her, "Mary, at least you're safe, said the man, it's me Vittorio."

Mary embraced him, but her face was terror stricken.

"Where is Victor," she asked, "what did you do with Victor?" "Mary, Mary, look at your face, and your hands have so many cuts! What are you going to do? You must get to a Doctor!"

"I'm all right I tell you," Mary said, "I want to find Victor, VICTOR, VICTOR, WHERE ARE YOU!" She shouted out the anguished call to her son.

Vittorio remembered vaguely that Victor and Guiseppe had escaped the doomed limousine from the other side. He started to search the wreckage on what had been the right side of the limousine. There was a crumpled body, lying inert with it's arms encircling something, beneath what looked like the door from the limousine. As he lifted the body away he could see that the man was beyond help, his face and part of his head was missing. He bent to examine the body more closely because he could see something else. The man had been trying to protect something when he died. It was the body of a young boy, it was Victor and he knelt to lift him free.

As he carefully lifted Victor from the dead man's grasp, the little boy spoke! "Mummy, mummy, where are you?"

"Here's your Mummy," said Vittorio, carrying him to Mary, "he doesn't seem to be hurt too badly, but he's had a terrible shock, he might have been knocked unconscious."

"Oh my poor baby," said Mary. "Where was he Vittorio?"

"He was lying over there, underneath that wrecked car door. He was protected by someone who had him cradled in his arms.

Whoever it was, was killed."

A policeman approached, "Please get into the ambulance quickly," he said "we can help you both in there."

Vittorio identified himself as a member of State Security, "I want to help sort this thing out," said he, "there's been a senseless act of terrorism here."

"Thank you Major," said the policeman readily recognizing the security pass shown by Vittorio, "we will need your help, but we have to identify the victims. That body over there for instance, where you found the boy. We don't know who he was at all."

"I don't know him," said Vittorio, "but there is a chance that this lady who is the boy's mother might know him."

Vittorio called Mary to him, "Please Mary could you go with this man and see if you can identify someone who is badly hurt over there? I'll look after Victor for you."

Mary reluctantly let Vittorio hold Victor in his arms while she picked her way through the wreckage. She instantly recognized the body by its clothing but when she looked at the face, what had been the face of Guiseppe Alamo she was sick. The terribly torn features and now the sickening smell of burning flesh over whelmed her completely and she collapsed in a dead faint. She was carried to the ambulance and remembered nothing of the drive in the ambulance to the hospital.

When she awoke in her hospital bed, Vittorio was sitting with her and Victor was asleep on the bed beside her. She looked from her son to his father, trying to orientate herself in these surroundings. Vittorio gently stroked her forehead with the palm of his hand to calm her fears. "Try to get some rest, my Dear, It's been a terrible ordeal for you."

"I can't, for thinking of that poor man on the pavement. Was it actually Guiseppe Alamo? Why would they do that to him?"

"He was a very brave man, Mary, I had no idea what he wanted when he came running out to the limousine. I just had time to push Victor down to the floor and out of the way, because I thought he wanted to get at me. Instead he grabbed Victor and jumped out of the other side of the car. He knew the explosion was coming and wanted to shield him.

"You'll be safe here in the hospital today Mary., and then probably we'll go to Boscolini's to spend a few days. I think it would be better than going back to that hotel.

"OOH, I couldn't face that hotel, ever again, Vittorio."

Vittorio knew instinctively that the attack was aimed at him.

He first got in touch with his chief in Rome to inform him that he was safe, but more important, to ask why this man Arturo had not contacted him yet. He remembered the black van which had escaped from the vicinity of the Rex Hotel so soon after the fire. He went back to the Relays Cerates to question some of the porters on duty at the time, and found one man who remembered a van exactly like the one he described, even to the license plate number, which indicated that it had come from the Naples area. It had carried three people to the hotel.

One of the men had gone straight into the lobby and the green slacks and sports shirt was exactly the clothing worn by the man who had rescued Victor at the cost of his own life. This must have been Guiseppe Alamo.

The porter had also recalled that one of the other men in the van had gone to look at the trunk of the Boscolini limousine. He had been acting suspiciously as if he were looking at the wheels. He had touched something underneath the limo. And then had hurried back into the van, got into the driver's seat had been joined by his companion, and the van had sped away out of the square. He was about to report these mysterious occurrences when the third man who had been in the lobby burst from the hotel door to try to stop the Boscolini limousine from moving.

Vittorio decided to keep this information to himself, rather than let the police look after the sordid details. He was contacted finally by Arturo, his man in charge of protection Arturo's men fanned out in a search of the city. Within 12 hours they were shadowing a black van with Naples license plates. The men in the van drove erratically around Florence for two days before heading south on the Rome road.

They drove five miles into the mountains when a road block stopped them. The two men from Naples, Tauro and his driver greeted their fellow Mafia with smiles, handshakes and the familiar Mafia hug as they alighted from the van. When they were invited back to sit in Arthur's car they suspected nothing, but when their own black van was pushed over a precipice they began to have some fear for their own safety. They were taken to the port of Oust to board Arturo's handsome yacht and their suspicions were somewhat allayed.

However as the yacht sailed out of sight and sound of land, they were both shot squarely in the middle of the temple, their bodies weighted with cement and tossed over board into the sea. It was a patented Mafia operation, and left the authorities no traceable remains. The police were told that the explosion had been a bungled Mafia vengeance coup and looked no further.

Arturo reported these facts to Vittorio and Vittorio at least could assure Mary that she and her son were safe from any further attacks.

Mary sent a large bouquet of flowers to Guiseppe's mother in Sorrento hoping to help her in some way with her grievous loss. Anna Alano would be devastated, as would any mother at the loss of her son. When Mary called to express her sympathies, she in turn was very distressed at hearing Anna Allano's reaction. Mrs. Alano placed the blame for all of her misfortunes on the shoulders of her daughter in law. "You were the unfaithful one, you were about to desert my Guiseppe, and it is no wonder that he tried to preserve his marriage. Marriage after all is a sacrament of our church, and not to be taken so lightly as you have taken it."

"We were all injured, even Victor had a close call," said Mary, and but for Guiseppe he would not be with me today. Victor and I must see you."

"Do you want to come back to Sorrento to live, then?" Anna asked the question hopefully, which seemed to indicate a softening attitude on her part.

"Why yes, Vittorio and I would—"

Anna did not allow Mary to finish the sentence for at the mention of the name Vittorio, her attitude immediately hardened, as Mary expected it would.

"How could you say that man's name to me now?" asked Anna. She was enraged. "The very man who murdered my son, God bless him."

Mary thought it best to talk another day. She said gently, "and God bless you, Mother," and hung up the phone.

Vittorio had been listening to parts of the conversation. "You were right my dear," he said, "it would not be the best time for you to travel anyway. At least until all those cuts have healed."

"I was thinking that perhaps Mother Alano should see what we have all been through, but that would have only deepened her sadness.," said Mary.

Mary arranged to move her factory to Florence in the following months.

She came back to the little English village of Harrowdale and she and Vittorio were married at last. Victor stood in the church for the wedding and at last the full story of their romance could be told. Mary pointed with pride to the resemblance between her son and her husband. Vittorio gladly assumed the position of chief of accounting in her businesses, replacing her father, who was more than ready to retire. He became the chief labor negotiator for the firm filling a position which had been largely ignored in the past.